EVERYTHING
BUT A GROOM

EVERYTHING BUT A GROOM

•

Holly Jacobs

AVALON BOOKS
NEW YORK

Published by Thomas Bouregy & Co., Inc.
160 Madison Avenue, New York, NY 10016

Library of Congress Cataloging-in-Publication Data

Jacobs, Holly, 1963–
    Everything but a groom / Holly Jacobs.
        p. cm.
    ISBN 978-0-8034-9864-8 (acid-free paper)
    1. Brides—Fiction.   2. Blessing and cursing—Fiction.
3. Erie (Pa.)—Fiction.   4. Domestic fiction.   I. Title.
    PS3610.A35643E94 2007
    813'.6—dc22

                                        2007026113

PRINTED IN THE UNITED STATES OF AMERICA
ON ACID-FREE PAPER
BY HADDON CRAFTSMEN, BLOOMSBURG, PENNSYLVANIA

For the Burhenns. To Mike and Eda
for making me an aunt to three of the most
special girls around, and especially Madison,
Sarah, and Regan, who truly light up my life.

Prologue
The Salo Wedding Curse

Vancy Bashalde was the most beautiful woman in the small town of Erdely, Hungary. She was the much-loved and cosseted daughter of the community's mayor, but she didn't think of herself as spoiled. It wasn't that she expected things to go her way due to some sense of self-importance or entitlement; it was simply that things *did* go her way, so why would she expect them to change direction?

When Vancy set her sights on Bela Salo—a carpenter with amazing skills and an even more amazing smile, a man who made her laugh, a man who she knew saw more than her physical beauty, who saw who she was inside, where it mattered—she wasn't surprised when he fell in love with her as completely as she loved him.

1

That's just how things happened for Vancy Bashalde.

Never had a wedding been planned with more care. It was to be the most elaborate wedding the small town of Erdely had ever seen. Vancy would walk down the aisle of the church to the man she loved, and they, of course, would live happily ever after.

When her wedding day arrived, the sky was bright blue, the sun beat on the springtime fields— everything was just as Vancy had planned.

Yes, her picture-perfect wedding day had arrived . . . but the groom, Bela Salo, hadn't.

Shamed in front of the entire town, Vancy held her head high and proclaimed Bela's desertion was for the best. She put on a good front, but she was brokenhearted. The woman who always had things go her way suddenly discovered what disappointment was. Even worse, she discovered what having a broken heart meant.

As she packed up the remains of her wedding that wasn't, Vancy uttered the words, "*I hope Bela never gets a big, beautiful wedding like this.*" As an afterthought she added, "*I hope that no one in his family does.*"

After all, if Vancy Bashalde, the pride of Erdely, couldn't have her big, perfect wedding, then neither Bela nor his heirs should have one.

It wasn't the thought of Bela's wedding that really cut her; it was thinking of Bela marrying some other woman. It was the thought of having to watch him love someone else, then someday having to witness their children marry and see him and this woman standing side by side, sharing a love Bela had obviously never felt for her.

As she calmed down, Vancy—who, despite her heartbreak, was still a hopeless romantic—realized what she'd done when she said those words out loud. In Hungary it was common knowledge that words had power and that magic did exist.

What if she'd set into motion a chain of failed weddings and broken hearts? She couldn't stand the thought of others suffering the kind of heartache she was. Even if Bela didn't love her— her heart broke all over again at the thought—she couldn't stand to think of him suffering the way she was suffering right now.

So she tried taking the words back but wasn't sure it worked. Just in case, she tried to lessen their impact. She went into the woods, so no one would overhear her and think she was going insane, and said out loud so that whatever power was listening would hear, *"If I can't take back the words cursing Bela and his family to unhappy weddings, then let me add that it wasn't my intention to curse Bela or his family to a life without marriage or love. Just no big weddings that mean more than love does. I'm afraid that's what happened to me—I thought more about the wedding than what comes after. So when the day comes that someone in his family cares more about love and marriage and less about weddings, then please, please let that break my curse.*"

Days later, Bela arrived back in their small town of Erdely. He'd been in an accident and hadn't skipped out on their wedding at all. Overjoyed—well, not overjoyed that he'd had an accident but rather that he was all right and still loved her—and relieved, Vancy didn't even consider trying for another big wedding. They found the local priest that very night and married immediately. Soon thereafter they moved to the United States, and Bela took his knowledge of carpentry and began a small specialty business that over the years grew into a large, family-owned construction company.

Salo Construction became well known and respected in Erie, Pennsylvania.

Vancy forgot all about her silly words until years later, when her children started to dream about weddings . . . weddings that never quite worked out.

Vancy became sure that her curse was at fault, and she hoped that if one of her grandchildren cared more about love and marriage than about a wedding, her curse would be broken.

Vancy was desperate to break the curse that she, in fact, started. She'd learned the hard way that words have power.

But no one should underestimate the power a guilty grandmother wields.

Chapter One

Vancy Salo had everything under control. She'd checked the weather forecast, and all of Erie, Pennsylvania's TV station meteorologists had solemnly promised her that tomorrow would be in the mid-seventies and sunny. Perfect June weather was the forecast.

But just in case they were wrong, she had tents put up in the backyard. The tents also served as insurance that none of the guests ended up with a case of sun poisoning.

Vancy had talked to Father Martin at St. John's, and he assured her he'd had a physical last week, as per her request, and had passed with flying colors.

But just in case, Father Jackson from St. Luke's was on standby.

She had doubles of everything.

Even two wedding cakes.

Vancy had the wedding dress she'd picked out but also had had her mother's never-worn wedding dress altered, and it was in her closet.

Yes, Vancy had tried to plan for every contingency, believing her grandmother's story just enough to worry that whatever could go wrong, would go wrong. After years of hearing her grandmother's stories about failed family weddings, she was convinced that it was best to be prepared.

Why, Vancy even had a fire station two miles away that she could move the reception to if there was weather so bad that the tents wouldn't offer enough protection.

Yes, the younger Vancy Salo had planned for everything. But that did little to comfort her grandmother, Vancy Beshalde Salo, affectionately referred to as Nana Vancy. And her grandmother was quite vocal about her frustration with her granddaughter's wedding plans.

". . . and I begged her to just elope with her Al and break the curse, but you know children these days. They scoff at the old ways, and not one of my grandchildren believes in the curse any more than my own children did."

"Nana Vancy," Vancy said, at the moment with more annoyance than affection in her voice.

Her grandmother was a force to be reckoned

with. Only four foot eleven and a half—she always added the half because she said with her shortage of inches, every half counted—she was a white-haired dynamo. She looked up as Vancy approached. "Vancy, sweetie, meet John Warsaw. He's a reporter and works for the paper."

Vancy pasted her business smile onto her face as she shook the reporter's hand. "Nana, John and I are well acquainted. He's the reporter who wrote that lovely piece on Salo Construction for the paper last month."

"Thank you so much for the invitation to the wedding," John said.

Vancy would have preferred honoring her grandmother's request for a small wedding, but the fact that she was a part of Salo Contruction, and that her fiancé, Alvin Michaels, was running for City Council, made a big wedding a business opportunity, as well as a chance to convince her grandmother there was no such thing as the Salo Family Wedding Curse.

Nana Vancy had told the story of her own aborted wedding, and the subsequent curse, so many times, Vancy knew it by heart. The whole family did. And Vancy, along with her brother, Noah, and sister, Dori, had been told all their lives that it was up to them to help break the curse because Nana Vancy couldn't go to her deathbed under the weight of future family weddings being destroyed. Whenever

Nana, an irrepressible woman who showed no signs of slowing down, issued that particular plea, she made it sound as if that deathbed were just moments away.

So although Vancy, along with the rest of the family, knew the story backward and forward, Vancy would prefer that a reporter didn't get hold of it. She could see the headlines now: *Family Curse Alive and Well in Erie, PA*. Not that the curse would be alive after today. Once she and Al said their vows and walked up the aisle together, her grandmother would be able to rest easy. But in the meantime it was best to separate Nana from any and all members of the press. "John, I hope you don't mind if I borrow my grandmother."

"Certainly. But, Mrs. Salo, I'd love a chance to talk to you more later."

"Why, certainly, young man." Nana Vancy winked at the dark-haired young reporter.

Vancy smiled back at John, then hurriedly led her grandmother away. "Nana, you were flirting with the man."

"Vancy, sweetie, your grandfather doesn't mind if I look at a pretty boy, as long as I don't touch."

Vancy moaned in harmony with her grandmother's laughter.

"Nana, I know the bride's supposed to be the one who's nervous, but in this case, we're all worried about you."

Nana's laughter immediately died. "Sweetie, I'm not nervous. I'm just so sorry you're going to have to suffer the pain of an aborted wedding." She looked up. "The sky is looking a little overcast, so maybe it's going to be a freak storm blowing in off the lake that does it in. I'm on pins and needles waiting to see just how the curse manifests itself and ruins your beautiful wedding. You should have eloped, like I said. Then we could have had a huge celebration for you afterward, with no fear of cosmic reprisals."

Vancy didn't know why she bothered to try to convince her grandmother, but she always felt obligated to have a go at it. "Nana, there is no Salo Wedding Curse."

Her grandmother shook her head. "Tell that to your mother. Poor thing didn't have a clue what she was getting into when she joined the family. 'There's no Salo Family Wedding Curse' is just what she said . . . until lightning hit the church, and it burned down to mere ash on the ground. I told your grandfather it was our fault, and Salo Construction rebuilt it at cost, but he complained a lot. I reminded him of the fact that I might have made the curse, but he's the one who missed our wedding and set things into motion. After the fire your mother came to her senses and eloped."

Vancy gestured toward the sky. "Notice the three lightning rods I've had installed around the property? We're fine."

Nana Vancy just shook her head, white curls shellacked into place and never moving an inch. "What about your uncle's wedding? He thought taking it out onto the water would save him, but the boat sank, sending his huge wedding party and all his guests right into the water."

"Thankfully, it hadn't left the bay yet, and everyone got off the boat before it was even half a mile from the dock," young Vancy pointed out. "But you'll note, we're getting married on dry land."

"I've spent years worrying about the curse, and I think that if you didn't care so much about the wedding, it would be fine and the curse would be broken, but you do care, don't you?"

Vancy nodded. It was the truth: she did care. The wedding was a great opportunity for Al to make connections that would help him win his Council seat, and it was good PR for Salo Construction as well.

"Yes, that's what I was afraid of." Her grandmother sighed as she surveyed the transformed backyard. "You care a lot about this big, fancy affair you've put together, despite my warnings."

"Of course I do. We've invited a lot of city officials. The mayor, the chief of police. And look over there—it's that cute, redheaded police captain."

"You shouldn't be looking at cute men," Nana Vancy said with a very prim and proper *tsk.*

"Nana, Al and I agree that, just like you and Papa, we can both read the menu, we just can't order anymore." She smiled, hoping the joke would ease her grandmother's nerves, but Nana continued to eye the sky worriedly, as if expecting a bolt of lightning at any moment.

"Nana, there are more than just city officials, there are important business leaders too. Our guest list is good for Salo Construction and good for Al's political aspirations. So, yes, I care. This wedding is about more than Al and I saying our vows. It's business. And though I'm not involved with the day-to-day aspects of the company, I do care about it."

"I know," Nana said with a sigh. "And I just want to say I'm sorry before whatever happens. I love you. You're my namesake, my granddaughter. I never meant to do this to you, or to the family, when I said those horrible, horrible words so many years ago."

"Nana, it's going to be fine. I've planned for everything. Nothing's been left to chance. In just a few short hours I'll be Mrs. Alvin Michaels."

Her grandmother sadly shook her head and kissed her cheek. "Just remember, I love you."

"I love you too."

The music should have started.
Vancy had on her perfect dress.

The local weather people were brilliantly accurate . . . the weather had remained just as gorgeous.

Everyone was waiting. Even her younger sister, Dori, had shed her work clothes and put on her lovely maid-of-honor gown with very little complaint. She'd also forgone her braid and hard hat and had her dark hair expertly styled.

Yes, everything was ready.

Where was the music?

Where was her father? He was supposed to be here, holding her hand and walking her down the aisle.

Vancy forced herself to remain calm. Her father wasn't known for being overly prompt.

She glanced at her sister, who was fidgeting in her finery. "Dori, you're going to have to go see where Dad is."

Dori, for once, didn't argue. Maybe she was simply on her best behavior because her mother and grandmother had both lectured her. Or maybe putting on a dress was enough to make her always-confident sister feel ill at ease. Either way, Dori just said "Okay" and exited the room.

Left momentarily to her own devices, Vancy paced until she caught a glimpse of herself in the mirror and tried to force herself to calm down. She decided that her sister was probably behaving because looking at her wild-eyed sister had scared any thoughts of misbehavior out of Dori's mind.

Moments later Dori was back, without their father, looking grim.

Vancy, who'd pooh-poohed her grandmother's worries, suddenly felt a bit sick to her stomach. "Dori?"

"He's not here. He just called and said he's not coming. He—"

Vancy could see the pain and worry on Dori's face. She reached out and squeezed her little sister's shoulder. "Don't worry, sweetie. I've got a contingency for even this. Go get Noah. If my father's not available, then my brother can walk me down the aisle. And if you can't find Noah, then I'm sure we can get Papa Bela to fill in. Where is Dad? Was his plane late?"

Vancy had told her father, Emil Salo—begged him, even—to put off this business trip until after the wedding. But did he listen?

No.

Salo men weren't known for listening. That's why Papa Bela had missed his wedding, and now his son was going to miss his daughter's wedding for the same stupid reason.

Dori remained rooted to the spot.

"Dori, go get Noah."

Dori shook her head and looked pale. "Vancy, it's not Dad. It's—"

Dori was interrupted by the door flying open and Nana Vancy running into the room, her eyes filled with tears. "Darling, I'm so sorry. I thought it would be some natural disaster. I never imagined your Alvin would leave you practically at the altar."

"What?" It was as if the sea roared in her ears, and the earth shifted under her feet. For the first time in her life, Vancy Salo thought she might pass out. "What?"

"You didn't tell her?" Nana Vancy asked Dori.

"I was in the middle of it when you burst in."

Nana gave Dori a dirty look, then pulled Vancy into her arms, giving her something to hold on to. "I'm sorry, *kedvenc.* Alvin sent a note. He's not coming. He said he can't marry you because he doesn't love you. He thought he loved you enough, but it turned out he didn't."

"He doesn't love me?"

"I could have lied, but it's like a bandage—it's better to just say all the hurtful things at once, rather than prolong the pain. He's run off with a waitress he met last month. I guess he forgot that he could look but not order after all."

Vancy Salo had planned for everything from natural disasters to wedding-day mishaps. She had plans and backup plans. She'd thought of everything . . . everything except the possibility that Alvin didn't love her and would run off with a waitress.

That thought had never occurred to her.

Chapter Two

Matthew Wilde hated being disturbed when he was working, so he had ignored his phone all morning, letting the answering machine pick up. After all, he'd taken today away from the office and his usual tasks in order to finalize this big proposal. He'd check his messages when he was done.

He was too engrossed in sketching the plans for this new garden space to stop. He could see every detail in his mind's eye. He loved it when he could envision exactly how a landscape should look, and he worked feverishly, trying to get it all down on paper before the vision disappeared.

When someone first rang his doorbell, Matt planned on taking the same approach he'd used with the phone—simply ignoring it until whoever

it was got the hint and went away. But when the po-
lite buzz turned into incessant, repeated buzzes, he
finally admitted that even his powers of concentra-
tion were defeated. Pushing back from the drafting
table in his home office, he walked to the front door
of his house, ready to read whoever the bell-ringer
was the riot act.

He flung the door open, ready to roar, when he
spotted the two children behind the wild-eyed
woman. "You're him, aren't you?" she demanded
in a less than friendly way.

"Him who?"

"Mark Wilde?"

Matt's heart sank. He'd played this scene fre-
quently in the past, some irate stranger reading *him*
the riot act for something his brother had done.
"I'm his brother, Matt," he tried, hoping that would
be enough to end this particular tirade before it
started.

The woman's frown, followed by a deep breath
he was sure she would need to vent her spleen in
its entirety, told him that he wasn't going to be
lucky enough to avoid anything.

"Oh, there's a brother, is there? She never told
me that. Just said the last name was Wilde, and the
moment I saw your picture in the paper, I recognized you from the photo she'd kept in the boys'
room, and I knew they were yours."

She'd read the interview he'd done with the

newspaper about Everything Wilde. Matt had been so pleased with the exposure for his company, but now he was regretting it.

"You look just like him." It was more of an accusation than a compliment.

"I'm his twin."

"Well, wonderful, then you're either their father or their uncle, and either way, I'm leaving them with you. That one's Chris, that one's Rick, though I don't know how you're going to tell them apart. They've been with me a week, and I still can't. There's all their stuff." She nodded at a small stack of boxes Matt hadn't noticed until that moment. "So there you go."

Matt had been shut up in his office all day, working on his project. He'd thought a few times about getting up and making coffee but hadn't wanted to stop. Now he wished he had, because maybe if he had some caffeine coursing through his system, he'd be sharper and better able to follow this conversation. "I don't understand."

"The boys are staying with you now." She patted them on their heads. "You boys be good for your father. I'm out of here."

"But—"

She stopped and turned.

Matt felt a big wave of relief. She wasn't just dropping off two mystery boys and leaving.

She reached into her purse and withdrew a

mangled piece of paper. "Here's the letter." It had seen better days. There were coffee rings on it, and a burn mark.

The woman turned and hurried toward a beat-up green VW Beetle.

"Hey!" Matt yelled.

"It's all in the letter."

The woman jumped into her rusty Bug and sped away.

Matt looked down at the two little boys on his porch. What on earth was he supposed to do now?

"Hi," he said. "I'm Matt. And you're Chris and Rick?"

Two dark-haired heads bobbled their agreement.

There *was* a resemblance, he realized. Dark hair. Brown eyes that bordered on black. The sharp noses, the weird dimple in the left cheek—that had always been the bane of his existence. Mark's too.

"Well, why don't you come on in, and we'll figure out something."

The boys silently entered the house and stood in the foyer, waiting, eyeing him warily.

"Did you have lunch?"

Both shook their heads no.

"Well, let's call and order some pizza, and then we'll figure out where to go from there."

He started herding the boys toward the kitchen. One of them stopped, turned around, and looked Matt in the eye. "Are you our daddy?"

There was vulnerability in the boy's eyes. His twin turned and watched Matt, waiting as expectantly as his brother.

"No, I'm sure I'm not. But it looks like I might be your uncle. So, for now, why don't you call me Uncle Matt."

The explanation seemed to satisfy them, and the boys allowed him to lead them into the kitchen. He set them up with paper and colored pencils while they waited silently for the pizza to be delivered.

As soon as they were busy, he opened the letter and read:

Dear Mark,

Here they are. I've tried and tried to get hold of you. The money you gave me ran out a long time ago, and I just can't handle this anymore. My mom's watching them until she can track you down. I had the lawyer draw up a piece of paper saying I don't want any parental rights. I've done five years—more, if you count my pregnancy, and I do count it. I can't do any more. I've got dreams of my own. It's your turn now.

~Passion.

There was a legal-looking document in the envelope as well, and it looked as if the boys' mom had indeed given her parental rights to Mark.

Matt looked at the boys, silently drawing on the paper he'd supplied.

How could someone just leave her kids like that?

Then the realization that his brother had obviously done just that made his stomach sink. Mark had given the woman, this Passion, money, then just walked away. Leaving it up to Matt to pick up the pieces once again.

The phone rang. Matt was almost afraid to answer it. He'd always found that bad things came in threes. But on the off chance it was his brother, he felt he'd better.

"Hello?"

"Mr. Wilde?" asked a woman's voice.

"Yes."

"This is Vancy Salo. I have a bit of a landscaping emergency."

Vancy Salo. He'd recently done a huge backyard overhaul for her for some big wedding. "Landscaping emergency?"

"Yes. I need you at my house, now." There was a hint of desperation in her voice, which didn't quite jibe with his impression of the woman. When they'd met to discuss the landscaping, she'd been calm, self-assured, and very clear about what she envisioned.

"But—"

"Mr. Wilde, I don't like throwing around my

family name, but I'm well aware of the fact that Salo Construction has hired you to landscape for us on a number of our biggest jobs. I'd hate to think our companies' congenial relationship would be damaged due to your lack of understanding this very real landscaping emergency."

He glanced at the two boys, who were still abnormally quiet. They were so well behaved, he was sure they'd cooperate while he took care of whatever this crisis entailed.

"Where do you live again?"

Vancy filled him in, and he hung up.

"Well, boys, after we eat our pizza, we have a job to do."

Within twenty minutes of making the call to Matt Wilde, Vancy felt foolish. It wasn't his fault that her wedding . . . wasn't. And it wasn't the beautifully landscaped backyard's fault either. Everything Wilde was the premier landscaping business in town. Salo Construction would continue to use them no matter what. Threats weren't a standard business practice for Vancy.

She was a lawyer. She dealt with the company's legal matters in a straightforward way. No threats, just facts.

Yet here she was, threatening a poor landscaper whose only mistake was that he'd made such a beautiful, romantic backyard design, and every time

she looked at it she was reminded of what she'd
lost—her dream wedding. That wasn't Matthew
Wilde's fault.

Vancy had worked so hard to avoid being a
bridezilla . . . and here she was, becoming just that,
well after the fact. Interrupting the poor man's
Sunday and demanding he attend to her needs—
threatening him, even.

Feeling beyond ashamed, she called back but got
his answering machine. "In case you're there and
not picking up—and I wouldn't blame you, I was
inexcusably rude—I just wanted to apologize and
tell you to please forget the entire phone call. Your
backyard design was—is—beautiful. Please just
chalk up my earlier call to stress, and don't worry
about coming out here. I'm sorry."

She hung up the phone, and it immediately
rang. She felt an overwhelming sense of relief. At
least she'd caught the poor man before he used his
day off to come out to try to appease her temper
tantrum.

"Hello, Matt. I'm so sorry—"

"Miss Salo?" a woman's voice asked. Not Matt.
Darn.

"I'm sorry. I thought you were someone else.
Let's start over. Hello. Yes, this is Vancy Salo."

"Miss Salo, this is Kimberly Mason with
WMTV. I read the society page yesterday, and then
the follow-up in the paper this morning, and I'd

like an interview with you on your wedding that wasn't."

"Pardon?"

"The Salo Family Wedding Curse is such a great human-interest story. I mean, your own grandmother cursed your entire family? None of her children got their weddings, and now it looks as if the grandchildren won't either? Left-at-the-altar stories are big, especially since that runaway bride one a few years back. That one caught the public's attention for weeks. Your story has the potential to go even further. I mean, it's certainly a unique twist."

The reporter spit out the words so fast that Vancy was sure she'd misunderstood. "Pardon?"

"So, what time would be good for you? And could you possibly try to arrange to have your grandmother join us? We can either do the interview at your home or here at the station. I don't suppose you'd want to wear the wedding dress for it? I mean, after all, you paid all that money for it, you might as well get some use out of it."

"Pardon?"

The woman's words slowly sank in, and rather than parroting the word *pardon* again, she simply hung up and went to porch and retrieved her Sunday paper.

The phone rang again, and she ignored it as she thumbed through the newspaper.

There.

Salo Wedding Curse Spoils Yet Another Family Wedding.

Long ago in Erdely, Hungary, a young bride was left at the altar, her dream wedding destroyed. She uttered a curse that the missing groom never have his dream wedding, nor would his future children have theirs. But it turned out the would-be groom didn't abandon her. . . .

Oh, no.

The byline read *John Warsaw.*

Vancy had been picturing horrible fates for Al since yesterday, and now she added John Warsaw to her fantasy. The two of them, dangling from a pirate's yardarm, hungry sharks circling underneath . . .

Her answering machine had picked up the last message, but the phone was ringing again.

Hoping it was Matthew Wilde, she answered it. "Hello?"

"Ms. Salo, this is Tony Marcus from the *National News Hour,* and—"

Vancy hung up.

The phone started ringing the second she set it back on the charger. She picked it up.

"Ms. Salo, I'm with *Entertainment This Week,*

and my assistant just handed me a clip from your local newspaper—"

She pushed the off button and wished for an old-fashioned phone she could slam back into its receiver. The phone started ringing again almost immediately.

Erie wasn't New York City. How on earth could a national news program have picked up on the story?

"Hello?" she asked tentatively.

"Ms. Salo, I'm from the AP, and—"

She hung up again.

The doorbell rang.

Oh, no.

She opened the door, worrying she was going to find a reporter and cameraman on her porch. Instead, she found Matthew Wilde and two dark-haired little boys bookending him.

Her embarrassment came rushing back. "Oh, Mr. Wilde, I'm so sorry. I called you to apologize, but you didn't pick up, and I left a message, then everything here went absolutely crazy. . . ."

She let the apology fade off in midsentence as a news van pulled into the drive and a man got out.

"Hurry, bring your boys and come in."

Matt glanced behind his shoulder and back at her, an unasked question in his expression. "Come on, boys."

They came in, and she shut and locked the door.

Half a second later the doorbell rang.

"Ms. Salo," Matt said, shooting her a look that seemed to question her sanity. "I'm not sure why I'm here or what's going on."

"Vancy. Call me Vancy."

"Matt."

The pounding on the door grew louder.

"Are you going to get that?"

She shook her head and waited, looking pointedly at the boys. "And these are your new assistants?"

Matt looked down, as if surprised to find two boys standing next to him. "Oh, these are my . . . uh, nephews, Chris and Rick."

"Hi, boys. I'm Vancy. And you look hungry."

"No, ma'am. He"—the boy jerked his head at his uncle—"fed us pizza."

"You're Chris?"

He nodded. "I'm one minute older than Rick."

"Well, if not food, maybe I could interest you in a Disney movie? I've got them all, so you have your pick."

"All?" The previously silent Rick sounded quite impressed at the thought of anyone owning all the Disney DVDs.

Vancy felt the need to clarify. "Well, I own all the ones that have come out on DVD. Come on." She took them into what her family referred to as her tiny living room, which she chose to think of as cozy. She made sure the drapes were closed, then set the boys up and returned to Matt.

"Ms. Salo . . ."

"Vancy," she corrected. "And I know you're wondering why you're here and what's going on. I originally called to ask you to undo the landscaping you did on my backyard. It only took me a few minutes to realize how psychotic I'd sounded, so I called back, but you were already gone. As for what's going on here, my grandmother was talking to John Warsaw"—even as she said his name, she added a few more sharks to her fantasy of the reporter's demise—"and told him an old family legend. He ran it in an article that's been picked up on a national level, and—"

Simultaneously the doorbell and phone rang.

She closed her eyes, wishing she was anywhere but here. She'd have to go away. Maybe go stay with Nana? No, if they had her address and number, they had her grandmother's as well and were probably even now hounding poor Nana. Okay, so maybe Nana started this mess, but Vancy knew her grandmother had never intended this. She'd have to call and check on her, though she was sure Papa Bela could handle the reporters. Then—

"Vancy?"

She opened her eyes and found Matt looking at her with concern in his eyes. She gave a little shake.

"Don't worry. It's all right. I just didn't want you to take the boys out to face whoever is out there now. Maybe you could pull your truck into the garage, load them in, and get out without the media bothering you? I'm so sorry I called you, so sorry you're here, and now I've pulled your nephews into"—she peeked out the window and saw three news vans—"into the midst of this zoo."

"I know how things can get beyond your control. Things you couldn't fathom in your wildest imagination. For instance, today I was working at home, when the doorbell rang and a woman handed me the boys and a note, then left."

"You weren't expecting them?"

He shook his head. "I didn't even knew they existed. I certainly didn't expect them to end up on my doorstep."

Vancy glanced into the living room, where the boys sat quietly watching a movie. "Their mother just dumped them on you?"

"No, it was their grandmother. Their mother had dumped the boys on her. Seems before that, my brother paid their mother off and left, without ever giving another thought to them. The poor kids have been abandoned by everyone. They got left with me minutes before you called."

"Oh, Matt, I'm even sorrier now that I had a little meltdown at your expense—sorrier than I was a minute ago." He looked so confused and so angry on the boys' behalf. "What are you going to do?" she asked softly.

He shrugged. "I don't know. I just don't know."

"There are agencies—"

He shook his head. "I might not have figured out much, but I know I can't just pawn them off onto someone else. Everyone in their life has abandoned them—my brother, their mother, and now their grandmother. I won't do it. I just have to figure out who I can get to babysit them tomorrow." The dueling bells rang again but barely even made him pause. "I have two projects I can't put off. And then I have to track down my brother." Another bell. "And—"

This time it was just the doorbell. He smiled. "But it appears I'm not the only one in an unexpected fix. What are you going to do?"

Vancy shrugged. "Thankfully, I have two weeks off from work. I thought I'd be on my honeymoon." She felt a twinge of regret that she wouldn't be sitting on a beach in the Bahamas as she'd planned. "So I can go hole up in a hotel for a while and hide from the press. The couple of calls I inadvertently took mentioned some runaway-bride story the papers ran with a few years ago. They seem to think a grandmother cursing her own family will have at least as much audience pull. I just have to hide out until they realize I'm not going to be interviewed. I'll put the family on notice not to say anything else, then sneak away to some hotel."

Matt's eyes narrowed, and he studied her speculatively. "Or . . ."

Vancy didn't know him very well, but she was pretty sure his current expression was one of smug happiness, as if he'd figured out something that delighted him. "Or?"

"Well, I know it's a bizarre idea, but maybe you could come stay with me and babysit the boys until I make better plans?"

Matt heard the words spill out of his mouth. He knew he'd said them but still couldn't believe it. The idea had sounded grand in his head, but, watching Vancy Salo's shocked expression, he didn't feel quite as brilliant.

As a matter of fact, he felt dumb as a rock.

"You want me to come stay with you?"

"I just thought that it might be a way for both of us to get out of our current predicaments. You'd have somewhere to stay until this news story blows over, and I'd have someone to watch the boys until I can figure out what to do."

He waited for her to say no. Waited for her to laugh in his face. He felt rather bemused that she seemed to be considering the idea. She toyed with a black curl, her blue eyes darting from him to the window. Maybe she was trying to decide which was the lesser of two evils?

He could see her eyes come back into focus as she nodded. "Yes, that might work."

If Matt had been surprised to hear himself ask her, it was nothing compared to the shock he felt as she agreed.

"Just give me a minute to throw a few things into a bag." She left him standing near the window and hurried down her hall.

What had he been thinking, inviting a poor-little-rich-girl—a lawyer, no less—into his home? As if he didn't have enough trouble cleaning up yet another of Mark's messes. How could his brother just discard his own children this way?

The boys were quietly watching the video. They'd been quiet since they arrived. Not that Matt could blame them. They had to be confused—scared, even. He'd have to try to fix that.

"Ready." Vancy had one small bag.

"That's everything?"

She nodded. "Oh, wait, no, it isn't. I'm assuming you have a DVD player at home?"

"Yes."

"Great." She ran back to her room and moments later returned with a canvas bag in her hand. "Boys, pop that DVD out, and let's pack up my collection. You can borrow all the movies while you're staying with your uncle."

"Vancy, you don't have to—" he started.

She cut him off. "I know. But if they're watching my DVDs, we can be sure they're watching appropriate shows. All my Disney movies are rated G, PG maybe on some, but still appropriate. Otherwise they're surfing the television channels, and who knows what they'll end up watching?"

With all the precision of a military officer, Vancy had the DVDs packed, an air mattress she extracted from the front closet, and her suitcase in tow, and she herded the boys to the garage door to wait while he backed his truck into it.

As soon as he was in and the door was shut again, without waiting for his help she loaded the boys, the suitcase, the DVDs, and the air mattress into the back, then got into the front seat. Rather than buckling herself in, she got down on the floor.

"Whatcha doing?" Chris asked.

Matt turned around, and both boys were staring at Vancy, curiosity in their eyes. It was the most expression they'd shown since he met them.

"It's like a spy game," Vancy assured them. "We're going to try to sneak me out of here without all the people out front realizing I'm leaving."

She turned to Matt. "I figure maybe we can shake them if they don't know I'm with you."

Matt nodded. "Ready, boys?"

A little less subdued duo of yes's echoed out of the backseat.

He refused to think about the absurdity of this day. It had started normally enough. Coffee, the Sunday paper, then working in his home office instead of going to Everything Wilde and driving around town inspecting his crews' work.

And now? He had two boys and a woman-in-hiding in his truck.

Matt refused to try to figure out what he'd do next. He had the next few days covered, with Vancy's help. That was enough. He'd take the rest of it step-by-step, not looking too far ahead.

"Let's go. Operation: Save Vancy is in progress."

He opened the garage door and eased the truck out. He was about to get out and shut the door, but Vancy said, "Don't bother," and pushed a remote control on her key chain.

He cleared Vancy's driveway and her street without incident. Vancy didn't stir from her position on the floor.

"Aren't you going to get up?" he asked.

"Let's give it a couple more blocks." She waited, then finally crawled up into the seat, buckled herself in, and straightened some imaginary wrinkles in her slacks. Then, looking all prim and proper, as if she hadn't just been hiding on the floor of his truck, she turned to him. "Okay, before we go to your place, I have to ask what, if anything, do you have for the boys?"

"Their grandmother brought them and the clothes

on their backs and a couple small boxes of stuff I haven't checked out."

"Do you have a spare bed?"

"A double bed and dresser in a spartan, at best, guest room."

She sat still for a moment, as if she were calculating something in her head. Then she nodded to herself and said, "Fine. Then before we go back, let's stop at Target. We'll get what we need."

Matt hadn't even stopped to wonder if he had everything he needed for two small boys, but Vancy obviously had and decided he didn't.

They drove up Peach Street to Target, and before he'd caught his breath, she had them all inside the store.

Matthew Wilde had done many things in his thirty years of life, but none of them left him prepared for what happened next. Shopping with two boys . . . and Vancy.

They'd barely made it inside when the boys suddenly pepped up in front of a video-game display.

". . . and Chuckie said that Yoshi was the best."

Chris looked stubborn. "I'd want Mario Brothers."

"But—" Ricky started to argue.

Vancy interrupted the argument, sounding not the least bit flustered by it. "Tell you boys what. If you both cooperate and help us get the essentials, maybe you can get a treat." Vancy grabbed a cart. "You'd better get one too, Matt."

Matt wasn't sure he liked the sound of that. After all, how much could two little boys need? "You think we'll need two carts?"

She laughed. "I had a younger brother. I'm trying to multiply him by two and . . ." She paused, looking as if she was indeed doing a complex math problem in her head, then smiled. "Chris, Rick, why don't you two get a cart as well?"

Three carts? Matt tried to remember when he and Mark were young. He pictured their bedroom, decorated with an outer-space theme, toys and books lining the shelves, the closet filled with clothes.

"Oh, wait!" Vancy cried, with a look of embarrassment on her face. "I should have asked how much you plan on spending. I don't want to insult you, but this could get pricey. I'd be happy to help—"

He cut her off and tried not to feel insulted, though he was pretty sure he wasn't successful at it. "I can certainly afford what the boys need, even if I'm not as rich as the Salos."

She looked taken aback by his vehemence. "I didn't mean . . . I just . . . I mean, you said this was surprise, and I didn't want to push your budget beyond its limit."

And just like that Vancy's embarrassed surprise

gave way to annoyance right before his eyes. He saw her expression change, her jaw sort of set, her eyes narrow.

On some people the expression might have been intimidating, but seeing Vancy ruffle in annoyance was sort of . . . cute, though he was smart enough not to mention that fact. "Listen, I didn't mean—"

"Despite what you think of my family, Mr. Wilde, we all live on budgets, on our own incomes, not off some big family trust. I know what it's like to stretch a budget beyond its boundaries. I—"

"Truce," he said, holding up his hands. "I didn't mean it, and I'm sorry. I'm obviously touchy today. This is not quite what I had in mind for my Sunday."

Her expression relaxed, and she smiled. "No, I'm the one who's sorry. I've had to live down the Salo family name for years. I went into law because I wanted to make it on my own. For years I refused to represent my family because I felt it smacked of nepotism, but then their lawyer made a stupid error that almost resulted in a lawsuit, and I realized that I was the right person for the job *because* they were family and I'd always look out for their best interests. But I made it on my own first."

The conversation ground to a halt as Vancy herded the boys to the clothing department. Matt followed them and watched her in amazement. He couldn't quite determine how she so easily figured out what size Chris and Rick wore. But when she did, she systematically began loading up the first cart with jeans, shorts, T-shirts, and one nice outfit each.

Then came underwear and socks.

Toothbrushes—he'd never have remembered those—and kids' toothpaste, which was candy-flavored rather than mint. The boys seemed pleased.

After that it was on to the housewares aisle, and plastic plates and cups went into the basket. Then footwear—sneakers, dressier shoes, and sandals.

Toys.

Books.

Paper, crayons, markers.

She asked about the state of his linen closet, which was apparently lacking, because next came sheets, blankets, and towels.

Which reminded her, and back they went to the clothing department for swimsuits, then beach towels. Two carts were filled; the boys' was still empty. She'd been right to insist on a third, because apparently kids, like pets, needed special foods. Chris and Rick's cart was soon filled with juice boxes, fruit snacks, raisins, and various other stuff that apparently little boys couldn't live without.

And then Vancy recalled that there was some new child-seat law in Pennsylvania that meant the boys both needed booster seats.

As amazing as it was to watch Vancy power

shop, what was even more amazing was the way she got the boys to open up with her.

"Hey, Vancy, I like fish," Ricky—at least Matt thought it was Ricky—chimed in.

"And I like ponies." If the fish boy was Ricky, then the pony boy must be Chris.

She soon knew their favorite animals, colors, flavors. Knew that one was a chocolate ice cream fan, the other liked chocolate and vanilla swirled.

And the way she handled them.

She didn't overload them with too broad a question, like, *What do you want?* She gave them easier choices. *Would you like the blue or yellow? . . .* whatever the item was.

He noticed other parents with kids who were crying and whining. Ricky—he thought it was Ricky—gave a token whine when she informed him there would be no dart guns, and Matt waited, expecting a full-blown tantrum, but instead, as the boy's whining escalated, Vancy gave him a look that silenced him instantly.

In less than an hour they were all back in the truck, the back loaded down with packages, and the two boys once again buckled in, but this time into their brand-new booster seats.

Matt glanced back and gave an appreciative whistle. "That was amazing."

"What?" She looked confused.

"How you got all that done so fast."

"Oh, that. There's a rational explanation. I hate shopping. I mean hate it. If I have to shop, I want it over with as quickly as possible, which is why I've perfected power shopping. I go in with a list and just get it done. Fast, quick, and as painless as possible. Even better, I shop online when I can. But the boys' needs wouldn't wait for online, so there was no choice but a power shop."

"But still . . ."

"It's just a matter of organization."

She looked so cute. Prim and pleased with herself. He couldn't help grinning. "Vancy?"

"Yes?"

"Thanks. I'd never have thought of everything."

"Oh, I'm sure that's not everything, but at least it's a start. My grandmother always teased that kids are expensive pets to keep. I think she's right."

He laughed.

She glanced into the back, then in a lower voice asked, "Speaking of keeping, what are you going to do?"

"Later. We can discuss my predicament later, when they're asleep. Maybe you can lend me a legal opinion?"

"Looks like they're almost sleeping now—"

"No, we're not," one of the boys grumbled from the back.

"Good," Vancy said, turning in her seat to look at

them both. "We're almost at your uncle's, and then we'll make dinner. Maybe you two will help me?"

They both chimed in their willingness to help Vancy.

Matt couldn't help admiring again how well she handled them. "Nieces and nephews?" he asked.

He glanced over, and she shook her head. "No, just a bit of logic. Since it's almost dinnertime, I'd say it would be a good idea to keep them up, so they'll go to sleep properly tonight."

"And just telling them to stay awake will do that?"

"No, but this might." She turned around in her seat. "Boys, do you know any songs?"

"We know one about a boa constrictor," one said.

"Why don't you teach it to me?"

There were many things in life that Matthew Wilde hadn't planned on. But riding back down Peach Street with a woman and two boys singing about getting eaten by snakes—well, this wasn't something he'd even remotely imagined.

But imagined or not, Matt had to admit, it was kind of nice.

Chapter Three

Monday afternoon, Vancy held the phone to her ear as she gazed out Matt's kitchen window. His backyard looked the way she'd always imagined an English garden would. Trees, brick pathways, and low walls, with beautiful flowers in interesting little groupings.

Looking out at it, imagining she was sitting quietly on the one small bench, felt so much more peaceful than this particular conversation.

". . . Nana, yes, I'm safe. I talked to Mom and Dad, and they're filling in the rest of the family, but I thought I'd better call you personally."

"Where are you?" her grandmother demanded over the phone.

"I don't want to say, but I'm safe and away from

the media's eye. That's one of the reasons I wanted to call you myself. I've warned the rest of the family, but I wanted to talk to you personally and ask you not to speak to the press when and if they call."

"Oh," was her grandmother's only response.

Vancy had a horrible feeling of foreboding. "Nana?"

"Well, Vancy, my *lányunoka*, you see, I started getting calls yesterday. The first one was from that very nice reporter, Mr. Warsaw, from your wedding. He wanted to know where you were, then asked me a few more questions about my curse. I didn't see the harm in answering, but . . ."

Vancy's heart sank. "He's going to print more, isn't he?"

"So I hear. He thinks the fact that I inadvertently cursed my own family interests his readers. That you are the family member my curse is currently striking makes you a big part of that story."

"Oh, Nana." A hummingbird flitted around a bush right below the window. The plant had big, orangey, trumpetlike flowers all over it. The bird moved from one blossom to another. Vancy held still, not wanting to scare it away, and wishing desperately that she could watch the small bird in peace. It was so much nicer than worrying about what her grandmother had said.

"Vancy, I've lived all these years knowing it's my fault, my stupid anger and pride, that ruined all my children's weddings, and now it's starting to strike my grandchildren. I feel so guilty, and it hurts me even more that I didn't just ruin your wedding, but your marriage."

"You didn't ruin it. Alvin and his bimbette did." Hummingbirds, gardens, flowers . . . they weren't distracting her enough. She'd lost Al to another woman, ruined her perfect wedding, and was now the object of a media frenzy and public scrutiny. Yeah, there was no way a hummingbird was going to distract her from all that.

"Well, it will all blow over." Her grandmother paused, then added, "Eventually. Especially if you just lay low. I should have realized and not talked to Mr. Warsaw. I won't make the same mistake again. You just stay where you are. I'm no reporter, but I imagine that it's hard to write a story featuring someone you can't find. The press will forget all about you the minute some nice actor gets arrested for drunk driving or the like. You know what they say, everyone gets his five minutes of fame."

"I think it's fifteen minutes of fame, Nana."

Her grandmother said something in Hungarian, then switched back to English. "Well, either way, *kedvenc,* it won't last much longer. And at least this has kept you from going right back to work, which is what I suspect you would have done otherwise. You take some time off, get your feet back under you."

"Nana, I'm fine. More fine than I should be," Vancy confessed, because she needed to voice the thought that was preying on her conscience.

Her grandmother zeroed in on her confession with the same intensity of the hummingbird on its orange flower. "What do you mean?"

A light breeze was playing across the lawn, blowing the plant just the slightest bit to the right. There was something soothing about watching it, just not soothing enough. "I mean, Nana, that if I really loved Al, wouldn't I be devastated? I keep waiting for the unbearable pain to hit, and . . . well, it hasn't. When Papa Bela didn't show up for your wedding, you were heartbroken, weren't you?"

"I was distraught. So angry, so sad, so . . . I went a little crazy, which is why I made that awful curse."

"I don't feel any of that." She'd searched herself again and again but couldn't find a trace of that sort of devastation. "I feel embarrassed that he left me like that, right before our wedding, in front of all those people. The family. Our business associates and friends. More than just embarrassed, I'm furious that he opened me up to even more public humiliation with this whole news debacle."

"Part of that is my fault too."

"Well, yes, but your imagined curse wouldn't have been newsworthy if Alvin hadn't left me like that."

"So you're angry and embarrassed?"

"But not devastated," she confirmed. A ladybug landed on the glass, bright and cheery. Vancy was feeling anything but. "My heart isn't broken. My life isn't over. I should be crying, but I'm not. And the fact that I'm not is depressing me."

"Then maybe . . ." Her grandmother didn't finish the question.

Vancy finished it for her. "Then maybe I didn't love him the way a wife should love a husband?"

"You're the only one who can answer that, Vancy."

"I know." And that was a shame. Her grandmother had always been a font of wisdom and happily shared her thoughts and opinions with the family, whether they asked for them or not. Mostly they didn't.

For instance, when Vancy was planning the wedding, and her grandmother kept warning her to remember that her relationship with Alvin was far more important than the ceremony . . . she wished she'd listened then.

And right now, she wished her grandmother would tell her what to do, what to feel, because Vancy didn't have a clue.

Instead, her grandmother just said, "Well, wherever you are, stay there. Take your time, and enjoy yourself."

Vancy snorted.

"Well, *enjoy* is a relative term. Just take the time to get your feet back under you. I won't talk to any more reporters."

"Thanks, Nana." Talking to her grandmother made Vancy feel better, though she hadn't really resolved anything. She'd still gotten dumped at the altar. Her pain and humiliation was still fodder for the public's enjoyment. She was staying with a man she hardly knew, playing surrogate mother, and taking care of two boys who weren't hers.

"Call me, though. I'll worry." Her grandmother was the worrier in the family. Her parents, her brother and sister, even her grandfather would assume she could take of herself. She'd always been Vancy, the reliable one. Only her grandmother had ever seemed to notice the huge cracks in her confidence that she hid underneath her can-do facade.

"I'll call. And I have my cell phone, so you can still call me as well."

"Have a good day, *kedvenc.*"

"Thanks, Nana. You too. And stay out of trouble."

Her grandmother only laughed for a reply, then hung up.

"Good morning," Matt said, walking into the kitchen. He was already dressed and ready for work. "You're up early."

She turned around and, realizing she was still holding the phone, turned it off and set it down.

"Can't help getting up early. Even on weekends, when I could sleep in, I can't. I've got this internal alarm clock that wakes me up regardless."

"Owning my own business, I could sleep in, but there's always so much to do that there never seems to be a day to just take off and do it." He started across the kitchen to the coffeemaker.

"I put the coffee on. I hope you don't mind."

He took a mug from a cupboard and poured himself a cup. "No. It's nice to come down and have it ready." He took a long sip and sighed. "Very good."

Vancy tried to ignore a frisson of pleasure that ignited as she watched him savor the coffee. "Uh." He stopped his little love affair with the mug and watched her expectantly. Vancy desperately tried to think of something to say. "Uh...you have meetings today?"

"Yes. The company is up for a huge project that could really put us on the map here in Erie." A look of concern etched his face. "Are you sure you'll be all right with the boys?"

"We'll be fine." She thought she sounded confident, which wasn't quite the emotion she was feeling. Vancy didn't have tons of experience with kids. Shopping for the boys hadn't been bad—most of her ideas had simply seemed logical. Even settling them into bed last night had gone smoothly, but mainly because they were exhausted.

But spending an entire day with them on her own? She was a little less sure of her ability to apply logic to entertaining two young boys.

As if he could read her concerns, Matt said, "I'll try to get back as early as possible."

"Like I said, don't worry. I have everything under control." Even as she said the words, she prayed she was right.

Matt worried about Vancy and the boys all day long. He'd checked in twice, and both times he'd been assured that everything was fine. But on the last call he thought he'd detected a note of something less than fine in Vancy's voice. But when he'd pressed, she bristled and assured him he could take his time, that she had everything under control.

He pulled into the drive at four and found Vancy sitting quietly on one of the redwood rockers on the front porch. He got out of the truck and hurried up the walk.

"Everything okay?" he asked.

"Did you ever hear the phrase, 'famous last words'?"

He nodded and sat in the chair next to hers. He loved sitting here, looking out at the expansive front lawn. The huge frontage of the property was one of the reasons it had appealed to him. It was on Front Street, a street that followed the contours of a cliff that led down to the bay front proper. Once, the view had been of factories and a less than beautiful bay front. In recent years, much of the industry on Erie's bay had given way to tourist attractions—a giant marina, an outdoor amphitheater that offered free summer concerts, a bikeway.

He could look out over his well-planned lawn, across the road, to the bay. Today there were at least half a dozen sailboats in sight, along with a couple of Jet Skis racing back and forth.

"Well," she said, her voice sounding shaky, "I've heard the phrase 'famous last words' many times, but it never so aptly applied to me before today."

The view was forgotten, and he turned to Vancy, who was looking slightly worn around the edges. "What happened?"

Rather than answering, she asked, "Do know you know that if you take vinegar and put it on baking soda, it makes foam?"

Feeling confused, he nodded. "Yes."

"A foam that sort of looks like lava, or would if you added some sort of red coloring to it?"

"Yes, I guess it would resemble lava," he answered more slowly.

"Well, someone, a very smug-about-her-abilities sort of person, thought the best way to entertain the boys would be to do a project with them. We made a papier-mâché volcano. It was messy, but no problem to clean up. The boys even helped me. After lunch they asked if they could play 'boats' in the kitchen sink, and I couldn't think of anything it could hurt, other than dampening some clothes, so I said yes. That was my first mistake. No, I take that back—the volcano was my first mistake. Leaving them alone in the kitchen was the second."

Trying to think about what could have gone wrong, Matt asked, "Did they flood the kitchen?"

"No. I put down towels, filled the sink with water, and gave them a bunch of small kitchen utensils to play with, then went off to finish setting up their room. I was almost done putting away the clothes when I realized it was very quiet. Very, very quiet."

Quiet sounded just fine to him, but from the look on Vancy's face, it wasn't. "Quiet's not good?"

"Well, a logical person would think it was, but something told me that maybe I should check on the boys, and when I did, I quickly decided that quiet where kids are involved is a very bad thing. You should probably remember that." She rubbed her temples, as if her head hurt.

Matt had an urge to take over, to massage what he was sure were her tense shoulders. Just to touch her. He wasn't sure why, and he certainly wasn't about to act on it, but the inclination was still there.

"Anyway," she continued, "I went back into the kitchen and found that the boys had decided splashing in water wasn't as entertaining as they'd thought it would be, so they decided to find something more fun—"

Her story was interrupted by the two boys running out the front door. "Hi, Uncle Matt."

"And I literally caught them red-handed," Vancy finished with a flourish.

Matt wasn't quite sure what red-handed misdeed they'd been up to, but as he caught sight of their hands, he said, "Oh."

"They knew about the vinegar and soda, and they found a container of red dye in one of your cabinets."

Both boys' hands were a pinkish shade of red.

"They decided to make lava," she clarified, just in case he was still foggy on the details.

Two dark-haired heads bent in unison. "We're sorry, Uncle Matt."

"Yeah, sorry."

Vancy nodded. "Me too. I should have watched them better. I'm sorry."

"Wow, you're all very sorry. I get it, but it's no big deal. It's just dye. It will eventually wear off their hands."

"I don't know that it will wear off your butcher block," Vancy admitted.

"And we ruined our clothes," Ricky said.

"Mommy used to say she didn't know why she bought us clothes, 'cause we always ruined them before we'd barely got 'em on."

Both boys looked so guilty. No, not just guilty, scared. Scared of his reaction.

Gently Matt said, "Clothes can be replaced, and I bet if we sand the butcher block, we can get the red out." He looked at the boys, trying to wear his most serious expression. "I'll expect you two to help fix it, since you made the mess."

One head bobbed up and down in agreement. "We'll help, Uncle Matt. Promise."

The other head started bobbing as well. "And we won't do it again."

"Fine. Next time you want to try an experiment, you ask. Now that we've settled that, why don't you both go inside and turn on one of Vancy's movies, and we'll be right in."

"Uncle Matt?" Ricky looked sort of pale. "Are you sending us away now?"

"Sending you away?"

"'Cause we made a mess," Chris clarified.

"Boys, come here." Matt took them onto his knees. "Listen, I know you just met me, that you don't know me well yet, so I'm going to help you out. I don't send people away because they make a mistake. You two are my nephews, and I promise, no matter what, you'll always, always have a home here."

"Always?" Ricky didn't look convinced.

"Always," Matt assured them.

"Matt, do you cross your heart, hope to die, stick a needle in your eye promise?" Vancy asked.

Matt nodded, then made the appropriate motions and said, "I promise."

The boys crawled off his lap. Vancy leaned down and kissed them both on the forehead. "Go watch a show. We'll all help Uncle Matt sand the butcher block in a few minutes."

As they went back in, slamming the screen door behind them, Vancy said, "That was sweet of you, but I think they're going to need to hear those words over and over again before they start to believe them."

"I don't mind reminding them."

"You're a very special man, Matt Wilde." She smiled at him, then grew more serious. "I'm so sorry about not watching them better."

"Vancy, it's just some clothes and a butcher block. No biggie."

"But you asked me for help, and I blew it. I was sort of cocky, sure that I could handle two little boys with no problem whatsoever."

"It's fine," he assured her again.

She didn't look as if she bought the 'fineness' of the situation, but she asked, "So, how did your day go?"

He laughed. "Better than yours. I got the new

job. I'll be landscaping practically a whole block in
the new Dogwood subdivision. I've done two of the
houses, and four other neighbors have hired me."

"That's great."

"Yeah, it is." He'd started Everything Wilde
with a shoestring budget and just himself. Between
the work Salo Construction had been throwing his
way, and now this huge chunk of a new, trendy
subdivision, things were looking less shoestringy.

"We'll make something special for dinner," she
offered. "I'd planned to have something ready for
you when you got home, but I just finished cleaning up the lava and needed a bit of a break."

"Why don't we go out?" At her skeptical look,
he added, "I can't imagine any of the reporters will
be looking for you with a man and two kids."

"You're sure? I mean, there might not be any
lava potential, but there are a lot of ways for two
determined boys to wreak havoc in a public
venue."

He laughed. "I'm willing to take the chance if
you are."

She grinned, which had been his intent. He rel-
ished seeing her stressed look fade.

"That would be nice," she finally said.

"I have to make a few calls first." He stood.

She followed suit. "I'll make sure the boys are
presentable." She paused, then asked, "You haven't
tracked down your brother?"

"Not yet, but I will." He walked into the house, Vancy at his side.

"You go make your calls, and I'll go check on the boys." She walked toward the living room. He could hear the murmur of the television.

"Hey, Vancy?" She paused and looked back at him. "Thanks."

She looked confused. "For what?"

"For helping me out."

"You're helping me, remember?"

He peeked into the living room and watched her settle on the couch next to the boys, then hurried to his office.

Vancy's air mattress was on the floor, her things neatly folded in her suitcase. He stepped over them and went to his desk. He'd already put out a few calls, but it was time to make a few more.

He'd tried Mark's cell earlier but got a message that the number was out of service. Now he called anyone he could think of who might know where Mark was. No one did, but he left messages with all of them to have Mark call him if they heard from him.

Finally he made the call he'd been dreading.

"Hello?" came a voice on the other end of the line.

"Hi, Dad, it's Matt."

"How's everything growing?" It was his father's standard greeting. He chuckled, just as he always did. Don Wilde considered himself quite the co-median.

Most of the time Matt would groan, which was guaranteed to make his father laugh even louder. But today he simply said, "It's about Mark."

His father's laughter died immediately, replaced by a huge sigh. "What he do now?"

Matt outlined the arrival of the twins and his attempts to find Mark. "Any clue where he might be?" he asked.

"We haven't talked in quite a while."

He could hear the pain in his father's voice. Every one of Mark's missteps weighed on their father, as if he felt Mark's problems were his fault. Matt wished he hadn't had to make the call, but his father deserved to know about the boys. "Any suggestions on where to look for him?"

"No. No more suggestions than to keep doing what you're doing. Mark will bottom out and come to one of us for help. He always does. But speaking of doing . . . what are you going to do with the boys?"

Despite his annoyance at his brother, Matt smiled, thinking about Vancy. "I have a friend helping out with them."

"I'd say I'd take them, but your stepmother would . . ." His father let the sentence die off.

Matt's stepmother, Marcy, wasn't what anyone would call motherly. She was nice enough, and they got along, but try as he might, Matt couldn't imagine her dealing with two young boys. She liked things orderly and neat. That definitely wasn't in the cards with the boys around.

"That's all right, Dad. They're settling in here. I don't know that it would be a good thing to uproot them again so soon. Their mother left them, now their grandmother. I won't desert them as well. They've got a home here as long as they need it."

"Would you mind if we took a trip to Erie to meet them?"

"You know you and Marcy are welcome here whenever you want."

"I'll talk to her. I'm not sure how she'll feel about coming. But one way or another, I'll be there. It just hit me, I'm a grandpa. I've been waiting for this for years. I know I made tons of mistakes with you boys—"

"You loved us and did your best. That was enough."

After their mother died, their father had sort of floundered. It had taken him a long time to find his feet, but he'd always done his best, and that had been enough for Matt. Unfortunately, it had never been enough for Mark. To be honest, though, nothing was ever enough for Mark. He had a chip on his shoulder and had always felt the world owed him more than he got.

"Thanks for saying that, son." His father cleared

his throat and added, "I'll plan on coming up as soon as possible."

"Anytime, Dad."

Before he could say good-bye, his father added, "I'm so very proud of you, son."

Though he was a grown man, his father's approval meant a lot. "Thanks, Dad."

"It's not fair that you're picking up the pieces for your brother again."

"I told him I wouldn't bail him out again, but this is different, Dad. It's not about Mark. It's about Chris and Rick. They're little boys. I can't just walk away."

"Well, like I said, I'm proud of you, son. I'll see you soon."

They hung up, and Matt leaned back in his chair. He couldn't blame his stepmother for putting the brakes on his father's bailing Mark out of trouble. She'd made it clear that she wouldn't tolerate any more of that.

Matt had stepped in after that, and he even went so far as to give Mark a job at Everything Wilde last year, hoping his brother could make a fresh start. But Mark hadn't come into work on time and went whole days without showing up at all. It got to the point where Matt couldn't afford to keep him on. The fight when he fired Mark had driven a wedge between them—a wedge neither of them had been able to remove.

Mark had gone his way, called home for money more than once, but Matt had stayed firm and said no.

After those first few calls, Mark had stopped.

Worrying about his brother had become a daily part of Matt's life, and, despite their estrangement, that hadn't stopped. Now, unable to track him down, he was more worried than ever.

He didn't know what his next big move was, but for right now he'd simply concentrate on moving forward. And right now that meant seeing to the boys' dinner.

". . . roared their terrible roars," Vancy read from Maurice Sendak's classic, *Where the Wild Things Are*. She paused, and Chris and Ricky obligingly roared. As she continued the story, they gnashed their teeth on cue, then wiggled their fingers in clawlike fashion.

As she reached the end of the book, she realized it might not have been the best choice for a bedtime story.

Note to self, she thought. *Only choose quiet stories for bedtime from here on out.*

Matt poked his head in the door.

"Uncle Matt! Uncle Matt!" the Wild-Thing–excited boys hollered, jumping out from under the covers and bouncing enthusiastically on the bed they were sharing in the guest room. They roared, gnashed, and showed their claws in a very untired fashion.

"Uh, isn't story time meant to settle them down before bed?" He jumped onto the bed and wrestled the giggling boys back under the covers, only to have them each climb out again, still roaring quite happily.

"I picked the wrong story," Vancy said loudly in order to be heard over the roars. "But I was going to offer to tell the boys a story my Nana used to tell me. But first they have to get under the covers and stay under them—quietly," she added for good measure.

"Will you stay, Uncle Matt?" Chris was snuggling back in under the covers, though not looking the least bit sleepy.

"Sure. I'll sit over here and listen to Vancy's story." He tucked the boys in, kissed them each on the forehead, then started to go to the chair next to the bed. Ricky stopped him. "Uncle Matt, Mommy and Grandma aren't coming back, are they?"

Matt came back to the bed and sat on the edge. "It doesn't look as if they'll be back soon, but they may come back one day."

"And you can't find our daddy?"

He shook his head. "But I promise you both this, no matter what, you always, always have a home with me. This is your home, and I am your uncle. I'm here. And I talked to your grandpa, my dad, before dinner. He's coming to meet you as soon as possible."

"We have a grandpa?" Ricky asked, a sense of awe in his voice.

Matt nodded. "He never knew about you. Neither did I. But now that we do . . ." He leaned over and planted dual kisses on their foreheads. "We love you."

Vancy's throat constricted with emotion. Matt meant it. The boys might be too young to recognize the reality of his promise, but she wasn't. He meant every word of it. Chris and Rick might not know it yet, but they'd found their home.

Vancy worked to force words past the lump in her throat. "I may not be your real aunt, but you've got me too. I'll always be here for you."

"Now." Matt stood and moved to the chair. "I think Vancy was going to tell you a story."

"One my Nana used to tell me. You see, when my grandmother was little, she lived in another country called Hungary. They had marvelous stories there. One of the ones I loved best was about the white stag. You see, there was a great ruler named Nimrud. He had two sons, Hunor and Magor. One day, they saw a great white stag. . . ."

She continued relaying her grandmother's story until two sets of eyelids began to droop.

She rose and started for the door. She knew without turning around that Matt was following her.

He shut the door most of the way, leaving it open a crack.

They went into the living room. "Nice work, Vancy. You have the touch."

She sank onto the couch. "Not quite, but I'm learning as I go. For instance, I now know that quiet stories are the only way to go at bedtime."

Matt moved a jigsaw puzzle and a fire truck onto the coffee table and sat next to her. "Have I thanked you enough for helping me out like this?"

"Have I thanked you enough for giving me a place to hide out?"

"How's the story going?"

"The media hasn't quite gotten the hint that I'm not going to play this game. Reporters have contacted my family, and I guess they interviewed my almost-groom's sister on one of the nighttime entertainment shows."

She paused, the enormity of the situation hitting her all over again. "The most painful day of my life is entertainment for the masses. Actually, it goes beyond that. My grandmother made that stupid curse because she thought the man she loved had abandoned her. It was the most painful time in *her* life. Pain. That's fodder for the media as well. What does it say about a country when other people's pain becomes a source of amusement? We're a nation of voyeurs. And I can't be too high-and-mighty, because before this happened to me, I followed other stories without thinking what it meant to the person involved."

"It's wrong," Matt said. Then he added, "I'm sorry."

Vancy forced herself not to angst about the situation. Sooner or later the press would take the hint that she wasn't going to cooperate with them. "It'll blow over. It always does." Wanting—no, needing—to change the subject, she asked, "But about your brother. Did you make any progress in locating him?"

"No. But not being able to track down Mark—that's not so unusual. Mark is . . . well, Mark."

"He's done this sort of thing before?"

Matt shook his head. "Well, no, I haven't had any of his children dumped on my doorstep before. But Mark's disappeared before, and God knows he's had his share of trouble before."

"I'm sorry."

"Me too. He's my brother, and I love him. But . . ."

"But it's hard to stand by and watch someone you love hurt himself time and time again."

He nodded.

"So what are you going to do?"

"I'm going to have to make the boys' legal status clear. You're a lawyer. . . ." The statement hung there, more of a question than anything.

"Different kind of law. I work with contracts,

business sorts of things. But I can make some inquiries."

"Maybe it would be better to wait until I find Mark. Because if you were to check, then tell me that legally I had to turn them over to social services, I wouldn't, and that might come back to bite me later."

He was quiet a moment, then added, "They've already been deserted by their mother and grandmother. By my brother too, though they don't remember him. I won't desert them as well. So, for right now, I'm going to go on the assumption that their mother's turning them over to her mother, who in turn turned them over to me, is legal enough."

Vancy knew that he was right, that those two little boys deserved to have someone care about them, to know that, no matter what, someone cared. And it was obvious that they'd found that someone in Matt. In her too. But he had to be realistic. "Eventually . . ."

"I know, eventually it will have to be settled. But before that eventuality occurs, I hope I'll have found Mark."

"And then what? Once you've found him, are you hoping he'll agree to take them?"

"That's a good question. My brother can barely take care of himself. I can't imagine him taking care of the boys."

"Maybe having them, knowing he's a father, would change him."

"From the letter their mother wrote him, he's known he was a father all these years and did nothing. I can't imagine that my knowing he's a father will change that."

"I'm sorry."

"Having you here . . . having your help . . . well, it matters. I appreciate it." He reached out and took her hand.

She squeezed his hand and smiled. "We're quite the mutual-admiration society."

"What do you say I pick up the remnants of the day's play and then we just veg in front of some mindless television show for a bit?"

"What do you say *we both* pick up and then veg in front of some mindless television show for a bit?" she countered.

"Deal."

They both got off the couch and started at it. Vancy had imagined what it would be like married to Alvin. But most of those fantasies centered around the wedding, the reception, and even the honeymoon, sunning themselves on some Bahamian beach.

She'd never really fantasized about what would come after. About the simple, everyday things, like doing the dishes and picking up toys strewn throughout a house. Even now, laughing with

Matt as they did just that, she couldn't imagine doing these things with Alvin. They'd dated for years, and she couldn't recall ever sharing the everyday minutiae with him.

They'd kept separate homes, separate schedules— schedules that included each other but didn't necessarily center around each other. They'd done their chores separately, never sharing a moment like this.

Matt tossed a soft stuffed dog at her, which she handily caught.

"Hey, what's that serious look about?" he asked.

"Just thinking, realizing a few things about myself I'm not sure I'm very pleased about."

"Such as?"

"Such as I chose a husband based on what I thought I *should* want. Someone with compatible skills and habits. Someone who was comfortable. Alvin and I dated for years, but we never really shared our lives. We never did this—daily chores— together. I was trying to imagine it, and I couldn't. I had no trouble picturing the wedding, but the day-to-day stuff? Even now I can't imagine how it would have worked. We never talked about it, never thought that far ahead. Did we want kids? Where did we see ourselves in a year, five, ten? How could I not know these things about a man I'd planned to spend the rest of my life with?"

The enormity of what she'd almost done hit her

like a piano on the head. How could they not have talked about those things? The wedding, the honeymoon, his campaign, her job . . . but nothing that really mattered.

"I'm sure the two of you would have worked it out," Matt said with far more certainty than Vancy felt.

"I'm not so sure. I wish I was. But to be honest, I don't know if I knew Al well enough to even guess what he would have wanted. I've been so mad at him—leaving me at the altar, making me the subject of public scrutiny—but maybe I owe him. If he hadn't walked, I would have—walked out of the changing room and right down the aisle into a marriage I'm not so sure now would have been a good one."

"But you loved him," Matt said.

She was still holding the stuffed dog, and she hugged it to her chest. "Did I?"

"Didn't you?"

"I don't know." It hurt to admit that. Rather than stopping there, she continued, "I'd like to think I did, but I have to be honest with myself. I was embarrassed the day of the wedding, I've felt hunted by the press, and I've been furious that he put me into that situation. But brokenhearted? I don't think so. And shouldn't that have been my primary emotion? Shouldn't I be devastated at losing the man I loved?"

"I don't know. It's been a long time since I've had a meaningful relationship."

That caught her by surprise. "Why?"

"I've spent years trying to build up Everything Wilde. I started on a shoestring, with ten thousand dollars, a degree in business, and a lifetime of loving growing things. Now I've got a crew, I've got big accounts, my company's a success, and fact is, I've gone out on an occasional date but nothing serious."

"We're quite a pair." She tossed the dog into the basket they were using as a makeshift toy chest.

"So now what?" he asked.

"A good movie? Even a good television show?"

"Let's give it a try."

After some channel surfing, they finally settled on a movie of the week. It was some doomsday sort of scenario, buildings blowing up, and the hero and heroine not only saved the townspeople but fell in love.

As they walked down the hall on their way to bed, Matt to his bedroom, and Vancy to his office, she said, "That was exactly what I needed. I mean, compared to Paisley, whose entire way of life was obliterated, my life seems much better."

He laughed as if she'd made a joke, but Vancy realized that she hadn't really been kidding. The world as she knew it wasn't coming to an end. Her family was healthy and, for the most part, happy.

And maybe the fact that her wedding wasn't might not be the tragedy she'd initially thought it. Maybe Al's leaving was the best thing that could have happened for both of them.

It was something to think about.

Chapter Four

Over the next couple of days, Matt and Vancy developed a rhythm.

Their day started early with coffee and the paper, then Matt helped Vancy get the kids fed. After that he headed out to work, and Vancy and the boys played their morning away. She felt as if she'd become an expert at hide-and-seek, and, much to their delight, Matt had brought home a wading pool and an assortment of water toys that were guaranteed to occupy the boys for at least an hour. After lunch the boys napped. Vancy had called her office and started doing some work from home during their downtime. After naps, more play, and Vancy started dinner.

When Matt got home, he took over entertaining

the boys and finished making dinner, while Vancy borrowed his office and got some more work done. After dinner, they all hung out together until the boys' bedtime.

The cadence wasn't something they set out to develop, but it worked smoothly. There was nothing big about what they did, nothing earth-shattering, but it meant something to Matt.

He hadn't anticipated the feeling that came over him as he pulled into the drive and knew there wasn't just an empty house waiting to greet him.

He liked having someone to talk to, someone who asked about his day and then shared hers. Stories about the boys and—very generally, so as not to break an attorney-client privilege sort of thing—stories of her projects. Her family's business comprised about half of her workload, and the rest of it was contractual sorts of things, most of which went right over his head. But she seemed to feel better having vented, so he smiled and nodded and occasionally asked a question.

Matt realized that they felt like a . . . family.

Something he hadn't had in a long, long time. Oh, he knew his dad loved him, but he wasn't as sure about his stepmother's feelings, so there was always this awkwardness hanging over them when they were together. And with Mark there was no real brotherly connection. He felt more like the parent of a wayward child, despite the fact that they were the same age.

So as he approached the house after work on Friday, he found himself looking forward not only to the evening, but the whole weekend. He walked in, fully expecting the boys to rush up and greet him, with Vancy close at their heels, but instead . . . nothing.

A wave of disappointment swept over him, but he pushed it aside and listened. He'd discovered that wherever the boys were, noise was sure to be close at hand.

He heard voices, but no one came running.

Matt hurried into the living room and found his father, on the floor, spreading a blanket between the couch and a chair. "Dad?"

His dad looked up and grinned. "Hi, Matt. Our tent collapsed, and I'm fixing it."

"Uncle Matt?" Chris poked his head out from under the blanket. Ricky's head stuck out a second later, next to it. "You're home. Did you see we got a grandpa? You were right—he's ours. He came to see us, and we made this tent, and he's going to stay the weekend with us, and Vancy said we could eat our hot dogs in the tent, and our grandpa set it up so we could see the TV from here, and . . ."

Ricky lost steam, but Chris picked right up for him. "And if we're really good, and you say it's okay, Vancy said we could let Grandpa have our bed, and we could sleep here, in the tent, but only if you say so, 'cause Vancy says it's your house and you're the boss."

Matt sat down, feeling as breathless as if he'd just finished a marathon. "It isn't my house anymore."

The boys looked concerned.

"It's *our* house," he clarified. "You both live here now, remember? And since it's all of ours, that means you each get a vote. I'm still the grown-up, and sometimes I'll have to say no, but I still want to hear what you want. So, do you want to sleep in the tent and let your grandpa take your bed?"

The boys' yes's were deafening.

"Well, then, I guess we've worked out the sleeping arrangements."

"Is that a yes?" Ricky asked.

"Yes." Matt nodded, grinning at their excited expressions.

More yelling commenced, enough that Vancy hurried out from the kitchen to check on things.

She stopped in the doorway, and her face lit up. "Oh, you're home."

Their eyes held, and for a moment, despite the fact that there were two boys excitedly yelling, and his father was crawling around on the floor securing the blanket-slash-tent, it was as if there was no one in the room but the two of them.

There was something about Vancy. Her dark

curls were escaping her ponytail, and her eyes practically lit up the room as she smiled. She was striking, though not exactly beautiful or even pretty. But there was an air about her, something that spoke of confidence but also of vulnerability.

Standing there, wearing a pair of jeans and a plain blue top, a towel tucked into her waistband, as if whatever she'd been doing was messy, she looked adorable.

"So you two didn't need me to introduce you," Matt said.

Vancy laughed. "Your dad and I managed that quite nicely on our own. Don and I spent some time visiting, then the boys monopolized him."

"I like your *friend*," his father piped in from somewhere under the tent. He'd put an odd emphasis on the word *friend,* and before Matt could puzzle it out, Vancy tossed a pillow in the direction his father's voice had come from. It landed on the tent, and the boys shrieked. His father's head popped out from the opening.

"And, like I've said before, Don, that's all we are." To Matt she said, "Your dad thinks we're an item." She turned back to his dad. "Don, you can just wipe that look off your face, and the thought out of your head. I explained my situation. I thought I'd be married this week. Still on my honeymoon, even. I have no thoughts of dating anyone else for a long time."

"Who said anything about dating?" his dad asked, laughing.

"Dad, that's about as funny as your 'How's everything growing' quips."

His dad just laughed harder.

Matt tried again. "I assure you, Vancy and I are not an item. We're not even friends. I did a job for her, but we hardly know each other. We're just two people helping each other out."

"Matt, I didn't raise you to be stupid. If you haven't made a move on her yet, you should. I can spot a keeper when I see one."

Vancy offered his father a smile, but Matt could see it didn't quite reach her eyes. Something had set her off, and, for the life of him, he couldn't figure out what.

Still, she forced a smile, and his dad seemed convinced as she said, "Hey, the *keeper's* standing right here and must point out that she has no wishes to be *kept,* so if you'll pardon me, I'm going to go finish dinner."

"Vancy, I'll help." Matt got up.

His dad laughed. "Boys, looks like your grandpa is already making trouble."

Matt watched his father crawl back under the blanket and pull the flap down, then followed Vancy into the kitchen. "What can I do to help?"

She slammed a knife down with more force than

it required to chop a poor, defenseless carrot. "I've got it under control."

Chop.

"But I'd like to help."

"The boys wanted to eat in their tent, so I'm just making hot dogs, chips and"—*slam*—"carrot sticks."

Matt didn't think of himself as overly astute when it came to figuring out the female race. They confused him at the best of times. He knew that Vancy was mad at him, that he'd done something to irritate her—he did understand women enough to know when they were annoyed. But, for the life of him, he couldn't think of what it could be.

He'd hardly walked in the door. How much damage could he have managed in such a short time? Maybe she was upset about something else? Best to find out. "Vancy, did I do something wrong?"

She stopped the knife in midswing and looked at him. He didn't quite see anger. It looked more as if she was hurt.

"Matt, I don't want you to think I was trying to build what we had into something more than it is. At first it was about convenience for me, about helping you while hiding out. But even though it's been a short time, I thought we'd become something more than just . . . what was it? *'Just two people helping each other out.'* I didn't think calling us friends was a huge exaggeration."

"It wasn't. I didn't mean—"

"You sounded as if you meant it. You sort of jumped all over it, trying to make sure your father understood we weren't lovers or even friends, just two business acquaintances who barely even knew each other."

"Vancy, I didn't mean it like that, I swear. I do think of you as a friend."

She sniffed. "A little too little, a little too late."

"Vancy?" Was she crying?

She looked up, and there were unshed tears swimming in her eyes, magnifying their deep blue color. "Alvin talked to the media today. He told them that he'd thought he could marry me, that we had a lot in common and it would be a good match, then he met his waitress and discovered what real love was, what it meant to feel passionate about someone else."

Her voice dropped to a mere whisper. "That wouldn't have been so bad, but he went on to say that I wasn't exactly the type to inspire that kind of passion. He called me a . . ."

"A what?" Matt was currently envisioning all the ways he could pound Vancy's stupid ex into the ground and not get into trouble with the law or, even worse, with Vancy.

"*Modern woman,* but not in a way that was a

compliment. He said I was more married to my career than I ever would be to any man, and no man wants to marry someone like that."

"Vancy." Matt reached out and awkwardly patted her shoulder. He wanted to hold her, to hug her, but after the way she'd been chopping that carrot, he thought a quick pat was probably wiser.

She twisted away from his hand. "No, no, it's okay. I know I'm not a *Father Knows Best* sort of woman. There's nothing wrong with that. Mom and Nana were happy staying home and raising a family, but I'd never be content to not work. I spent years in school studying hard to earn my degree, and I like what I do. If that makes me modern and married to my work, so be it. At least my work won't run off with someone else and leave me standing at the altar." She sniffed again.

Matt was used to seeing a problem and fixing it, whether it was with his business or with his family. But this, watching Vancy suffer like this, made him feel totally useless. Other than tracking down her ex and punching him, there wasn't much he could do.

"Vancy," he said softly.

"No, no, I'm fine." She looked up, and he could still see unshed tears shining brightly in her eyes.

She offered him a wan smile. "I'm sorry. I shouldn't have snapped at you. I know I was overreacting. *Am* overreacting. It's just that I found out about the article, then your dad showed up, and it's been so crazy, I didn't have a chance to work through it, so I snapped at you. I'm sorry. You shouldn't have to play my whipping boy after a long day at work."

"And I should have chosen my words more carefully. We were just acquaintances at the beginning, but you're right, these last few days we've become so much more. I don't know what I'd do without you, and even after we've figured out what to do about the boys' situation, and the media has decided your grandmother's curse isn't all that newsworthy, I'll still want you in my life. You are a friend. A good one."

"Thanks. I think I really needed that." She seemed to give herself a good mental shake, smiled, and said, "Now, I believe you were offering to help me with dinner?"

"What do you say I take that knife and finish cutting the carrot sticks?"

She smiled. It wasn't her normal light-up-her-whole-face variety of smile, but it was a lot better than tears.

"Nervous?" she teased.

"Distraught women with sharp utensils can make for a messy situation."

"You have experience?" She was still teasing, still smiling. No more tears.

Matt felt a huge sense of relief. "My dad did.

Not a knife, though. A woman he briefly dated and a fork."

"Ow."

"Ask him to show you the scar on his hand."

He continued to kid around with Vancy, hoping it helped her forget about her ex's comments to the media, if only for a while. Matt generally considered himself a pacifist, but right now he wasn't feeling the least bit pacific toward Vancy's almost-husband. What on earth had she seen in the man?

Vancy's ex and his brother.

Matt would gladly kick either one's ass . . .

"As soon as I can," Vancy promised her brother, Noah, on the phone. He'd called to say he had some papers that needed looking over for Salo's.

Her brother had phoned her cell just as she finished the dishes. He sounded concerned, which made his grilling easier to handle. "I wouldn't have asked, but since you're not on your honey—" He must have realized that talking about her honeymoon might remind her about her wedding that wasn't, so he cut himself off and switched gears. "Nana said she'd bring them over, that she knows where you're hiding."

"I'm not hiding," Vancy assured him. "Well, not really. I'm just staying with a friend, waiting for things to blow over with the media."

"That sounds like hiding to me," Noah said softly.

"What do you know about being left at the altar, everyone you know and love gathered around— everyone except the groom? How can you understand my position, Noah? You've got someone you love, someone who would never do anything like this to you." His fiancée, Julianna, was kitten-cute with her pretty, blond good looks. They'd been together forever, it seemed, and Vancy couldn't imagine her ever hurting Matt like this.

"I know, I'm a lucky man." There was something in his voice that sounded less than happy at his luckiness.

"Is everything okay?" Vancy asked.

"Just fine. Don't try to change the subject."

"Listen, Noah. If I'm not ready to face the press and don't relish the whole the-bride's-own-grandmother-cursed-her-wedding story line, you have no right to imply that I'm a coward."

"Oh, Vancy, that wasn't what I was implying."

She knew her brother far too well. "Noah." She added more than a touch of warning to her tone, trying to emulate her grandmother's.

"Okay," he said, giving in. "Okay, that's exactly what I was implying."

She laughed, knowing she'd have to remember to thank Nana sometime for teaching her that particular inflection. Vancy had used it on clients before, and now it had easily done the trick with her brother.

"Noah, I have my reasons."

"So maybe the fact that you're hiding out took me by surprise. I mean, I fully expected you to give the press the bird and tell them where to put their story."

"That's really what you think I, a representative of Salo Construction, should do? Flip off Alvin and the media? I'm sure Mom, Dad, Dori, Papa, and Nana would agree with you that losing my temper on a national level would be wonderful for the family business."

"That's not what I meant. No literal flipping off, just some nicely timed and worded buzz-offs."

"Noah, as much as I'd love to go on television and rebut Alvin's statements, I won't. Alvin's opinion of me doesn't matter. The family matters, and since Salo Construction is an offshoot of the family, it matters. I won't put it in danger with reckless conduct that would serve no purpose other than to mollify my slightly bruised ego and feelings."

"Sometimes it's okay to do something without thinking it through, without planning it down to the nth degree."

"Well, I guess you could say I've done just that, since right now I'm supposed to be on a honeymoon, and instead—" She cut herself off.

"I'm your brother. It's all right to tell me where you are. I won't talk to the media."

It wasn't that she didn't trust Noah, but, knowing her brother, he might question her judgment when it came to her decision to stay with a man she only knew on a business level. She'd question someone in this bizarre situation too, if given just the dry facts. So, though she might understand his potential concern, that didn't mean she wanted to deal with it.

"Noah, I know you wouldn't breathe a word of it, but, truly, I prefer to be on my own, with no family members potentially dropping in on me."

"But Nana knows where you are."

"Not because I wanted her to, but because she's Nana. She can pry a confession out of any of us without even breaking a sweat. Have you ever been able to keep anything from her?"

He laughed. "No."

"Well, there you go. I managed to keep my whereabouts to myself through three of her phone calls. I thought that was pretty good. She's been bugging me to let her come visit, so if you send the papers with her, I'll be killing two birds with one stone. I'll go over them ASAP."

"Okay, then. And thanks, Vancy. I appreciate it."

"It's not like I have anything better to do." Well, that wasn't exactly true. Right now, as she spoke to her brother, she noticed that the living room had become strangely quiet. Disturbingly quiet.

"Uh, Noah, I've got to go."

"You're sure you're okay?"

"I'm fine. Maybe more fine than I should be, given the situation."

"So you're not pining away over the rat bastard?" he asked.

"No. And you'd think I would be, wouldn't you?"

"He was never good enough for you."

It was still too quiet. How long had she been in here doing the dishes, then with this phone call? Too long.

"Thanks, Noah. I think there's a chance you're biased, but that's okay, I appreciate it. But right now I've really got to go. Talk to you tomorrow."

She hung up and hurried out to the living room, not sure what she'd find. Granted, Matt and his Dad were out there, but still, you'd think with four men, there would be some noise.

She peeked into the living room and found Mr. Wilde cuddling Ricky, and Matt holding Chris, all four glued to the television. Whatever they were watching had them all smiling, and as she watched, something funny must have happened, because they all burst out laughing.

Matt's arm was snug around Chris, and he reached out and messed Ricky's hair. And watching him, so happy, surrounded by his family, her heart sort of melted.

The boys had come to Matt unexpectedly,

deserted by the only family members they'd ever known. They might still be confused and were most assuredly still hurt, but they were lucky. It might be years before they realized just how very lucky they were. But Vancy knew. Because when Rick and Chris had arrived on Matt's front steps, they'd come home.

Despite the fact that her life was more than a bit of a mess right now, she knew that she had that going for her—a loving family. Okay, so her grandmother had leaked her curse on the family to the media and precipitated this fiasco Vancy currently found herself in, but even with that, Vancy had no doubt that her grandmother loved her.

And a family that settled for nothing less than true and everlasting love. Nana and Papa Bela, her mother and father—even Noah had Julianna, a woman who would never betray him, never leave him standing on his own. Aunts. Uncles. Young cousins who someday would inherit Nana's attempts to break her curse. They could all drive her crazy, but, truth was, she recognized how lucky she was.

She must have sighed, because suddenly Matt looked up and caught her eye. "You coming in, or are you going to just going to stand there all night?"

"Come sit in the middle, Vancy," Ricky called.

"Yeah," Chris echoed.

Vancy grinned. "I'd love to." She squeezed into

the center of the couch. "So what are we watching?"

"*Chitty Chitty Bang Bang,*" Chris said excitedly.

"They'd never seen it. Can you imagine?" Matt started humming.

"Now that's just wrong," Vancy assured them all.

"They're on the beach, and the bad guys are coming," Ricky said nervously.

"It will be fine—you'll see," Vancy said.

Somewhere about the time the kids in the movie were being sung a lullaby by Dick Van Dyke, Vancy got up and made a bowl of popcorn. As she sat there, sandwiched between two men and two boys, Vancy felt a sense of belonging. The only other place she'd ever felt it was at home, with her family. But here, with four virtual strangers, she felt an echo of the same feeling.

When the movie ended, she helped tuck the boys into their makeshift bed for the night inside the tent.

"Can we have a story, Vancy?" Ricky asked.

She nodded. "I'll get a book. We're going to ask Uncle Matt to bring us some more, because we've almost exhausted our supply."

"No, not from a book," Chris said. "One of Nana's stories."

She sat next to the opening of the tent, two dark-haired heads propped on pillows by her thighs.

"Now, in Hungary, there are many stories about white storks, or as my grandmother called them, *fehér góyla*. My grandmother says that her family had a stork family that lived on the roof of their house. Each spring the people of Erdely celebrated and welcomed the storks home. My grandmother's grandmother, Eszti—whose name meant *star*—named her family's stork János, and one spring he didn't come home when the rest of the storks arrived. Eszti watched and waited, and finally, two weeks later, he landed in the yard, as if he didn't have the strength to land on the roof. My grandmother remembered the stories of how children's singing could make someone better, so she called all her neighborhood friends, and . . ."

Vancy continued the story about how Eszti and her friends had healed János, and how year after year first János, and later his children, lived on the house.

"I think they're out for the count," she whispered as she and Matt tiptoed out of the living room and into the hall.

"You're a natural at that."

"You're doing okay as well," she said, smiling. "Have you heard from your brother?"

"No. I've called everyone I can think of, left messages for him with all of them."

"Do you want me to make inquiries about your legal rights? I don't know how long you should continue in this legal limbo. What if one of the boys were injured? You don't have any legal rights to sign a medical release. And I know it's a few months a way, but what about enrolling them in school this fall?"

Matt nodded. "I've thought about those things as well. And if I can't find him soon, I'm going to have to do something, but I'd rather wait awhile longer."

"Do you think your father might want the boys?"

"No. We talked some this afternoon, and though he's thrilled to find out he's a grandfather, he's not in the position to take them. His wife . . ." He shrugged. "She's not exactly motherly, or grandmotherly. I'll confess, I don't know Marcy well, but he said she didn't seem very thrilled to find she was a grandmother, albeit a step-grandmother."

"Is the fact that he doesn't want custody a good thing?" She clarified, "I mean, do you want to keep them?"

"I don't know. I don't think that Mark's going to . . ." He shrugged. "I just don't know. I'm not really set up for kids. Right now it's working because you're here, but eventually you're going to go back to your own life, and then what? I don't know what to do, but I can't imagine just letting them go."

"You'll figure it out." She put a hand on his shoulder. "You'll figure out what's best for both you and them."

He sighed and looked tired. Down-to-the-bone exhausted. "You sound so sure."

"I am. You're a good man, Matthew Wilde. And you care about those boys. I'm sure you'll find the best place for them."

He reached out and took her hand. "Thanks. You've made this all so much easier. I don't know what I'd have done without you."

The hand he was holding tingled, as if it were asleep, zinging in a not unpleasant way. Vancy wasn't sure what the feeling was, but she could probably go on holding Matt's hand for quite some time, even though it was making thinking difficult. What had he said?

Something about her making this easier, thanking her?

She tried to formulate a response. "Well, I do know what would have happened without a place for me to hide out. I'd be fodder for some tabloid headline. So I owe you thanks as well. And, truth be told, I'm having a blast with the boys. I haven't enjoyed myself so much in years."

There. That sounded pretty good. Pretty coherent. As if the fact that he was touching her wasn't fogging up her brain.

Matt's dad poked his head out the boys' door. "Hey, are you two going to spoon in that hall all night, or can you let a man get a bit of sleep?" He slammed the door shut.

"Why do I feel like a teenager whose parents are flashing the front porch light?" Vancy whispered with a giggle.

"Were your parents flashers?"

She snorted at the statement. "Not to my knowledge."

He blushed. "That didn't come out right. It was poor terminology on my part."

She laughed all the harder.

In a very prim and proper voice he said succinctly, "Did your parents flash the porch light if you and a boyfriend spent too much time saying good night?"

"I did know what you meant, but you've totally ruined my night's sleep. I'm not going to be able to shake the mental image of my mom and dad naked underneath trench coats." She giggled some more. What was it about Matt that had her feeling young and giddy?

"Porch light?" he prompted.

Still chuckling, she answered his question. "My father would have been a porch light flasher, I think, but my mother kept him in check."

"I'd like to meet them," Matt said.

"Well, meeting the Salo family isn't for the faint of heart. They're . . ." She searched for the right word. "Original."

This time he laughed. "I think I'm up for it. And I'd like to sometime. I know Dori, since she's on-site so often when I work with Salo, and I've encountered Noah on occasion, but I don't think I've ever met your parents or grandparents."

"Well, my grandmother's coming over tomorrow, so you'll get your first dose. Just don't say I didn't warn you."

His father ducked his head out of the boys' room again. "Just kiss the girl, and get it over with." Laughing, he shut the door again.

"He thinks we're—" She stopped, not sure how to end the sentence.

"I tried to explain about your not being in a good place for a relationship. That you're just walking away from almost getting married."

"I'll confess, I don't know that I gave the forever part of it much thought. I mean, I was going to marry Al. I spent months and months planning the wedding down to the smallest detail, but in all that time I don't know that I gave much thought to anything beyond the honeymoon. We had decided he'd move into my place, but nothing more. Where did we stand on kids? Where did we hope we'd be in ten years?" She shrugged. "No clue."

"Do you think you want kids?" Matt asked.

"If you'd asked me before all this, I'd have been indifferent at best, but Ricky and Chris have shown me that I definitely want to have kids. Lots of them. I know I'll mess up, but look how much I've already figured out."

"No loud stories at bedtime," he said with a smile.

"No leaving them unsupervised in a kitchen, hide all dyes and indelible markers, and if things get too quiet, it's probably not a good sign. And that even if little boys protest, they still like being kissed good night."

"Little boys aren't the only ones who like a good-night kiss."

Vancy wasn't sure what to say to that, what to do. Matt was still holding her hand—or maybe she was holding his? There was definitely mutual holding. And the tingle was still there, letting her know how very much she enjoyed the sensation. But kissing?

"Kiss her!" his father called again, this time without opening the door.

Before she knew what she was doing, Vancy leaned forward, inviting Matt to do just that.

And Matt leaned forward, his free hand still at his side, and gently touched his lips to Vancy's. They were so soft and inviting. It was a sweet introduction of a kiss. Their lips brushed each other's, and then he pulled back.

"Should I apologize?" he asked.

"Should I?"

"Why don't we both not worry about apologies and go to bed. I've always been an early riser, but the boys have given *early* a whole a new meaning."

"Good idea." Vancy started down the hall toward his office, then turned around. "Matt, I know I'm on the rebound, that I shouldn't have kissed you—"

"I kissed you," he felt the need to clarify.

"And I know it's too soon, but even if I apologized, it would be a lie. I'm not sorry at all." And with that, she opened the office door and ducked inside.

Matt was grinning as he walked to his own door. He wasn't sure why. His life was a mess. He'd inherited two boys and wasn't exactly sure where he stood legally with them. He couldn't find his brother. He'd kissed a woman who most surely was on the rebound. And if his father was here, there was a chance his stepmother would follow.

Not exactly a run-of-the-mill week.

But he'd just kissed Vancy Salo, and, truth be told, he was pretty sure he'd do it again the first opportunity that presented itself.

His life might be crazy, but if Vancy were around, that wasn't such a bad trade-off.

Chapter Five

"They remind me of you kids when you were that age," Nana Vancy said on Monday afternoon.

Reporters had kept her away for the weekend, but she'd assured Vancy that she'd been cautious and hadn't seen any sign of them this morning.

She'd brought Noah's files for Vancy, along with some egg-and-potato casserole. It was a Hungarian dish her grandmother always made if someone need comforting. And Vancy figured she qualified.

It wasn't just the left-at-the-altar thing, or even the chased-by-the-media thing. There was an entirely new element to her current state of turmoil, which she'd come to think of as the kissed-Matt thing.

Multiple kisses.

There was an especially tender one on Saturday. Vancy had been ruminating that it was exactly a week from her almost-wedding and feeling rather blue, when all of sudden, there was Matt, kissing her, and all thoughts of anything but him fled.

Yes, they'd snuck more than their share over the weekend. It was tough with two little boys and one new grandpa underfoot, but they'd managed admirably.

The one thing they hadn't managed was discussing just what all that kissing meant. What they both wanted it to mean.

She had no idea what she was doing and even less of an idea why kissing Matt seemed so much more appealing than kissing Al had ever been.

Which is why the egg-and-potato casserole was exactly what she needed right now.

"Thanks, Nana. This is delicious, as always," she said as she scooped up another bite.

"I wasn't sure the boys would be impressed. They didn't grow up with my cooking. Which is why I brought the cookies too."

Sitting in Matt's sunny kitchen, eating casserole with her grandmother, made Vancy feel centered, not quite as adrift as she'd been feeling. She eyed the bag of cookies. "Uh, I might love the casserole, but I'll confess, the cookies will make a great dessert."

"I know my girl and her sweet tooth." Nana grew serious. "How are you really, *lányunoka*?"

"I'm fine." That was the problem, wasn't it? But she wasn't about to tell her grandmother that, so she changed the subject. "So, any more contact from the press?"

"I've almost forgotten about them. They didn't bother me at all yesterday."

Vancy felt a palpable sense of relief. "New week, new story, maybe?"

"Maybe. I don't understand how they thought my greatest sorrow, cursing my whole family, made for a good story." Her grandmother took a sip of her tea, wearing a perplexed expression.

"People love other people's misery," Vancy explained between bites. "So not only was it a bride jilted on her wedding day, but it was also a grandmother cursing her whole family. Two miseries for the price of one."

"Well, I didn't find it very entertaining." Nana took another sip of tea, then leaned toward Vancy. "I tried to tell you that you needed to scale back the wedding and put more thought into the marriage than the ceremony—"

"But I wouldn't listen. I don't think I ever even heard what you were trying to say, but I understand now. It's too late, but I get it."

"Do you?"

Vancy nodded. "Looking after Rick and Chris, I realize that I like kids, that I want to have a bunch. I never really thought that far ahead with Al. And to be honest, I don't think he did either. Our wedding wasn't a celebration of love—it was a business opportunity for me, for Salo Construction, and for Al. It shouldn't have been."

Her grandmother reached across the table and patted her hand. "Ah, *kedvenc,* I'm so sorry you had to go through the experience, but I can't say I'm sorry that you figured that all out. I made the same mistake at the wedding your grandfather missed. But by the time he came back, I had decided what was important, and a big wedding didn't seem to matter any longer. Being with your grandfather, my Bela—that was what I wanted. We've lived all these years together, moved to a new country together, so young and so ready to spread our wings. We raised a family here, built a business together. That's what I remember, not a wedding."

"I—"

Rick and Chris burst into the kitchen. Ricky yelled, "Vancy, Vancy, Vancy, hurry! Some witch is in the front yard chasing our new grandpa."

"Yeah," Chris said, his eyes wide. "She pulled up in a big black car. Maybe witches can't use brooms in the daylight? She's yelling at him an' chasin' him. Do you think she'll turn him into a toad if she catches him?"

"And if she does, can we make him a cage and catch him flies?"

"No, I don't, so there will be no fly-catching."

"If she does turn your grandfather into a toad, I'll turn him back before he's hungry enough to need flies," Nana promised the boys. "Did I tell you boys that I have Gypsy blood in me? And a Gypsy can outdo a witch any day of the week."

"Cool. Gypsies beat witches." Chris accepted her grandmother's proclamation without argument.

"Then hurry, Nana," Ricky said. He grabbed one of her hands, then Chris grabbed Vancy's, and both boys pulled them into the front yard. Indeed, an older woman, who didn't *look* overly witchlike in her pink Chanel suit and expertly coiffed hair, was out there. And as they drew closer and heard her voice, Vancy agreed she had definite witch leanings.

". . . and then those urchins you're claiming as your grandsons, though I think that's a foolish assumption to make until your son has some sort of official DNA testing, threw this at me." She held a rather dirty-looking ball.

A ball Vancy knew had been in one of the shopping carts last week but that now looked as if it might have spent a decade out in the elements.

"Wow, what did you both do to that ball?" she asked the boys.

"We made a dirt stew," Chris answered, as if that explained everything.

". . . and just look at this mark on my skirt." The witch pointed to a smudge on the Pepto-Bismol pink skirt. "And look at this yard. It's a broken heel just waiting to happen."

"No one told you to come here, Marcy."

She stopped her complaining and looked affronted. "Of course, I came. You're my husband, and you're here."

"We talked about this."

Vancy cleared her throat, and Matt's father and the witch, who'd just admitted to being Matt's stepmother, turned and faced them.

"Who are you?" the witch—Vancy gave herself a mental shake and substituted *Marcy*—asked, narrowing her eyes and studying Vancy with the same intensity she'd been giving the spot on her pink skirt moments before.

Vancy forced what she hoped was a welcoming smile. "I'm Vancy Salo. And this is my grandmother, Vancy."

"Vancy and Vancy. How quaint." Marcy looked anything but impressed.

Vancy's smile felt more brittle, but she kept it in place. "And you've met the boys. Chris and Rick."

"Oh, yes, we've met." Marcy pinned them with a rather witchy glare. "Are you responsible for them? If so, young lady, let me assure you that I'd withhold your paycheck if it were up to me, because you're obviously doing a very poor job of it. These miscreants—"

"She's a friend of Matt's, and she doesn't receive a paycheck. And even if she did, we couldn't afford to pay her enough for the wonderful job she's done. And, as I said, the boys and I were playing catch, so this is my fault, if you're looking to place the blame."

Don Wilde had struck Vancy as an easygoing, goes-with-the-flow sort of man, until that minute. He stared at his wife with anything but an easy look.

Marcy visibly blanched. "I . . . Well, I . . ." She drew a deep breath. "Well, I'm sorry. Boys, come say hello to your grandma."

The boys screamed and hid behind Vancy and her grandmother.

"I think the boys have had all the salutations they can stand for the day. If you don't mind, I'm going to take them inside, clean them up, and get them ready for a nap."

"We don' need a nap, Vancy," they said in unison.

"Ah, but if it were nap time, you'd need a snack, and it just so happens that Nana brought cookies. And I bet if you don't kick up a fuss, we can talk her into giving you a nap-time story. You know the one I told you last night? That was one Nana used to tell me when I was little. She's got a million, and she tells them oh, so much better than I do."

Chris peeked out from behind Vancy and looked at her grandmother. "Would you tell us a story, Nana?"

Ricky peeked out from behind Nana and added, "Our old grandma never told us stories."

"Or made us cookies."

"She just yelled at us that she didn't know why she had to take care of us, that our mama should've."

"She was kinda scary, just like the witch."

As Vancy led them indoors, leaving Don to deal with his wife, the boys went on telling her and her grandmother bits of the life they'd led, and each word was like a dagger in her heart.

It was obvious that even when their mother was around, she'd been as careless with the boys' feelings as their grandmother was. It made Vancy want to sweep the twins into her arms and hold them tightly, never letting anyone or anything hurt them again.

She realized that she didn't have that right.

But Matt did.

And at that moment Vancy knew that she'd do whatever it took, whatever she had to, to see that Matt had all her help, anything she could give, to keep these two boys from any further pain.

She was sitting mulling over just how she could make that happen as Nana told the boys a story about her best friend, Jolan, and her escapades, when she heard Don and his wife calling her.

She rose. "Nana, would you excuse me a moment?"

"We'll be fine." Her grandmother shooed her away.

She leaned down and kissed the boys' foreheads, and her heart melted. She loved them. It was that quick and ultimately that simple. And she'd do whatever she needed to do to keep them safe and, more than that, happy.

She hurried out to the living room and found Matt's dad and stepmother staring out the window.

Marcy tugged the curtain aside to give Vancy a better view. "There's a news van out front."

"Matt told me about your problem with the tabloids, and I have to say, I'm pretty sure they've found you," Don added.

Vancy's heart sank as she saw the van parked in the drive behind Marcy's and her grandmother's cars. "It's been over a week. I thought—well, I'd hoped—that they'd forgotten about me, about the story."

"I guess you were wrong."

Vancy couldn't decide just what Marcy's expression was as she said the words. Smug? Sympathetic?

"Now what do I do?" Vancy bowed her head and

rubbed her temples. She thought she'd shaken the press, thought she was past this. All she'd done was bring the media to Matt's.

It had been a rhetorical question, but Marcy answered, "Listen, I know Don thinks I'm without any practical talents, but this I can handle."

Vancy looked up, still unable to read Marcy Wilde. "What do you plan to do?"

"You just stay here and watch." With that, Marcy stormed out the front door.

Vancy leaned close to the glass, trying to hear what Marcy was saying.

Don was more direct. He simply opened the window.

". . . and this is private property. How dare you bother an old lady with your silly cameras? I know the media is curious about how I, a former Miss Arkansas, ended up so far from home, here in the wilds of Erie, Pennsylvania. I mean, I'd grown accustomed to the bright lights of New York City and LA, and I find it surprising myself."

"Ma'am, we're looking for—" a very brave reporter started.

Marcy cut him off. "Believe me, I've had problems with the press hounding me for decades, young man. I know all your wily ways. But when I got married, I put my beauty-pageant past behind me, along with the start of a very promising television career. I'm sure you've done your homework and realize I was the face of Mystic Cleanser. So I understand why you're here, but I don't want you media hounds digging it up again, so just move your little news truck and find a better story."

The cameraman looked confused and not just a little intimidated. He took a step backward, trying to put distance between himself and Matt's stepmother. "Ma'am, I'm sure the fact that you were Miss Arkansas—"

"And the face of Mystic Cleanser," Marcy added.

"Right. You were Miss Arkansas and the face of Mystic Cleanser a long time ago. And I'm sure some people would find it of interest—"

"A long time ago?" she repeated. "A long time ago?" Her voice had risen both in volume and pitch.

"You're the one who mentioned decades," the hapless cameraman pointed out.

"Young man, I know that the younger generation missed out on their manners lessons, so let me assist you. A lady may mention whatever time period she wants in regard to herself and her age. Any gentleman worth his salt would know that not only should he hasten to deny she could possibly be that old, but he should also refrain from using words like *a long time ago* in any sentence that centers around her."

The cameraman nodded. "Yes, ma'am."

"Now, you were saying?" Marcy folded her

arms over her chest and waited, tapping one of her slight marred, designer shoes.

"I . . . uh . . ."

"That's what I thought. Now, just get back into your little van and back it out of this driveway. Go find a real story. I heard that somebody out in Wattsburg had a bear in the backyard."

"But, ma'am, we got a tip that the cursed bride is hiding out here."

"Listen, I've already told you that I'm not interested in your writing a piece on me."

"Ma'am," the man tried again. "I think you're confused."

"Hah! Don?" she called into the house.

He grinned. "That's my cue." He hurried out the front door into the yard. "Yes, dear?"

"Did you unload my luggage as I asked?"

"No, darling."

Marcy gazed at the now sort of nauseated-looking reporter. "See, if there was ever a cursed bride, it's me. And as I've stated, I'm not willing to give you a story. I don't want the rest of the press to start hounding me again. So I'd like you to leave."

"But, ma'am . . ."

Even from the window with a sheer and a screen between them, Vancy could see Marcy's icy glare and knew *she* wouldn't be brave enough to stand in its way.

"I believe you were leaving, young man?"

"Yes, ma'am."

"And if I see this news crew anywhere in the vicinity of my stepson's home, I'll be calling the police."

"Ma'am, after dealing with you, the police don't sound all that intimidating."

She patted his cheek, and he flinched. "Why, that's the nicest thing anyone's said to me today. Now be on your way. And Don"—she turned and looked at her poor husband, straining under the weight of her three cases—"give me one of those before you give yourself a heart attack, because I'm not going to spend my time trying to nurse you back to health because you were too stubborn to admit you're getting old."

She turned back to the reporter. "Cursed bride. Yes, you've got that right."

And she ushered Don back into the house.

As she came in, she faced Vancy and her grandmother at the window. Vancy was amused and relieved to see that the news van was backing out of the driveway.

Marcy walked up to Vancy. "We didn't officially meet out in the yard. I'm Marcy Wilde, and you must be Vancy, the one causing all this trouble."

Vancy nodded. "Yes, ma'am."

"And you're the grandmother who cursed your own family?"

Nana, never one to back down, stood to her full four feet eleven and a half inches and said, "Yes."

Marcy thrust out her right hand. "Now, that's a story I'm looking forward to hearing. But first, I believe, I have some grandsons to meet. Of course, that is, if I'm assuming correctly that you don't allow filthy balls inside the house?"

"I don't," Vancy assured her. "But they're napping."

"Fine, then you can make your grandmother and me a cup of tea, and she can tell me how it came to pass that she put a curse on her own family. And you . . ." She pinned Don in her line of sight.

"Yes?"

"You can give me a kiss and tell me you're glad I came."

He laughed. "You're an amazing woman, Marcy Van Houghton Wilde."

"I know. I'm possibly a cursed bride if ever there was one, but you, my dear, are the luckiest of grooms."

Chapter Six

"It's almost too quiet," Vancy whispered to Matt later that night as they sat side by side on the couch.

"Is there such a thing as too quiet?" Matt asked in a normal speaking voice.

"Shh!" she warned. "You might wake them."

He laughed. "The boys are dead to the world. Moving the tent to under the dining room table was a stroke of brilliance. It would take a stampede to wake them, and even then I'd have my doubts."

"I wasn't worried about the boys. I worried about waking your father and your stepmother. I didn't think we'd ever get them settled down for the night. The whole we're-grandparents excitement certainly kicked in after dinner."

109

Matt was grinning. "I've got to confess, if you'd told me last week that I'd see Marcy sitting on the floor laughing with two boys as they watch *Shrek* . . . well, I wouldn't have believed it. I've never really spent much time with her. I thought I had her pegged. I guess I should have known there had to be some reason my father fell for her."

Despite her rather brusque demeanor, Marcy had definitely won them all over. She'd started to win Vancy's approval with her handling of the press, but she'd totally won Vancy's heart when she slowly warmed to the boys. Vancy realized it wasn't that Marcy didn't care, it was just that she had a hard time showing her feelings. Vancy's family tended to be very open with their thoughts and feelings— sometimes too open. Marcy wasn't wired that way. And she had even less experience with kids than Vancy did. But once Marcy got started, she was even more hesitant to call it a night than Chris and Ricky were.

"Yesterday, if you'd told me that I'd be battling to get a fifty-something-year-old to go to bed instead of the boys, I wouldn't have believed it." Vancy smiled.

Matt shook his head. "I still don't believe it. She really did seem to have fun. Dad too."

She'd offered to let the boys take her air mattress and sleep on the couch, but Don had insisted he wanted a chance to camp out. "You're sure your dad's going to be okay sleeping on the floor with the boys?"

"He'll be fine. He's having a ball."

"Matt." *Say the words,* she commanded herself. *Say the words.* Slowly, with difficulty, she managed, "Maybe it's time for me to think about going home."

Her heart sank even as she said the words. Truth was—a truth she wouldn't admit out loud—she didn't want to leave, and she was trying to figure out why.

After all, she had a great job, a job she was good at and loved. Not everyone was that lucky. And she had a family who really loved her. Of course, she'd almost married a man she hardly missed at all. She wasn't sure what that said about her, but she was sure she was going to miss what she'd found here at Matt's.

She'd miss the boys.

And, though she hated to admit it, she'd miss Matt.

She didn't want to leave.

And because she didn't want to, she knew she should leave, sooner rather than later.

She forced herself to keep going. "I mean, you obviously have enough help here now. Your dad and Marcy can take care of the boys, so you don't need me."

"Oh." He was silent a moment.

Vancy was generally good at reading clients, but she couldn't read Matt. Was he relieved she was leaving? Or maybe, just maybe, was he feeling something less than enthused? Maybe he'd miss her?

Finally he nodded. "I understand. I knew you couldn't stay."

This time she was the one who nodded. "It was just a short-term solution to an unexpected set of problems."

"Speaking of unexpected problems, are you sure it's okay for you to go home? You're sure the press is done with the story?"

"Well, Marcy certainly sent them on their way today."

"Yes. She was magnificent, but you won't have Marcy if you leave. I probably won't even have her here long."

"Oh?" She tried to maintain a serious expression, but thinking maybe Matt still needed her made her want to smile. She brutally suppressed the urge. "I thought they were staying. I mean, Marcy even told the boys their bedtime story tonight."

"She didn't want to be outdone by your grandmother." He dropped his voice to a conspiratorial whisper. "And don't tell her, but your grandmother's stories still win, hands down. I wouldn't say it to her, but I don't think her story about her best shopping day at Bloomingdale's is going to beat your grandmother's stork tales. The boys told me they want to go with their *nana* to Hungary."

Hearing that melted Vancy's heart. She knew her grandmother would be pleased as well. "She loved getting to spend time with them. She's been lobbying us for great-grandchildren. Since it's obviously not going to happen anytime soon for me, my brother, Noah, is her next likely candidate. He just got engaged."

"Hey, you'll find the right guy."

"I don't know. Maybe there is no right guy for me. Maybe I'll just consider myself married to my job."

Matt put an arm around her shoulders and drew her close. She knew he was only trying to comfort her, and it was working. Wrapped in Matt's arms, her head pillowed against his chest, all her anxiety and fears melted away.

"Listen, I know right now you're upset, but you'll feel better soon, and you'll find the right guy and go on to have dozens of kids."

With her ear pressed against him, his voice made a rumbling sound that made her smile. Then she registered what he'd said.

"Dozens?" she squeaked. She raised her head so she could look him in the eye. "As in twelve?" She snorted. "I was thinking two or three."

His eyes were dancing, and she knew he'd been teasing. Even though she was sitting up, he kept his arm around her as he assured her, "Well, I could see you with dozens, but I guess just a couple is all right too."

"After dealing with Chris and Rick, I think two is a perfect number for a lot of reasons. Each has a built-in playmate, someone to help keep him entertained, while you still have a hand for each. And if you're reading to just two, you can have one on either side, and both can see the book. I mean, if you had a dozen, how would you manage to read to them? There'd always be a huge fight over who got to see the pictures."

He laughed and held her tighter. "I can see that you've given this quite a bit of thought."

She nodded. "Just recently. Al and I hadn't really talked about kids, and I'll confess, I hadn't really considered them. My focus was on the wedding. But now, since being with the boys? I can't stop thinking about having some someday, and if I never find the right man, I think not having kids will be what I regret the most."

That was the truth, but not the whole truth. The whole truth was, she didn't want some as-yet-unknown children, she wanted Ricky and Chris. She wanted to tell them their bedtime story every night. She wanted to listen to their stories. She wanted to watch their delight with something as simple as a tent built over a dining room table to sleep in.

Leaving was probably the wisest course. It would

hurt to leave them, but how much more would it hurt if she stayed longer?

She looked at Matt, and she had to confess, it wasn't just Rick and Chris she'd miss.

It was him.

This man sitting next to her, holding her, trying to comfort her. There was something about Matt Wilde that touched her. She hadn't asked it to, hadn't wanted it to, but there it was.

She wanted nothing more than to stay here in his arms.

"Vancy? I feel the same way."

For a moment she was confused, thinking that he was saying he wanted to continue holding her, but then she realized he was talking about the boys. About having kids.

"I've been so focused on my business that I've hardly even dated, but now, because of the boys, I realize my life needs more balance. I want a family."

Even more softly he added, "I want the boys. And I'm scared to death that Mark's going to try to take them. If I thought he'd step up and really take care of them, it would be hard to let them go, but I'd manage. But I don't believe he can take care of them, and if he takes them, I'll worry."

"Do you want me to start making those calls?"

"And what if you find out and tell me I need to turn them over to an agency?"

"You have them. You took them when no one else wanted them. That's something."

"But it might not be enough." He was quiet a moment, as if weighing his options. "If I don't find Mark by Friday, then you can see what we need to do."

"But you'd want custody?" she pressed, needing to know, willing him to confirm that he did. She would go crazy worrying about them if Mark took them. But if they were with Matt, she'd be able to let go, even though every fiber of her being wanted to stay with the boys.

To stay with Matt as well.

"Yes, I want custody."

Hearing him say the words was just what she needed. She hugged him, then realized what she was doing, and released him and tried to be all business. "How will you juggle them and work?"

"School starts in September. That will help. And I'll just have to juggle my schedule until then and find someone to watch them for the times I can't."

She just nodded. Part of her wanted to say she'd take the boys when Matt couldn't. That between school and the two of them juggling their schedules, they could make it work. But she didn't say it. She didn't have the right. She was just a temporary babysitter.

"Well, I'm sure your dad and Marcy will stay

until the end of next week. Like I said, you don't need me here."

"Vancy, you're wrong."

For a moment she thought he was going to kiss her, but instead he pulled her close and hugged her. "I do need you, Vancy. Rather, the boys do. They've been through so much upheaval. It will hurt them if you just suddenly leave. You still have this week off, right?"

She nodded, her head pressed against his chest and feeling so right there.

"I know it's asking a lot, but could you see your way to staying through Friday? If I haven't found Mark by then, you'll start checking what my best legal course would be. And we can tell the boys tomorrow you're going home on Friday, so they'll have some time to adjust to the thought."

A reprieve.

Oh, it was a short reprieve, just a few extra days, but Vancy felt a million times lighter. "Are you sure? Your quiet house is suddenly being overrun by people."

"Yes. I'm sure. Very sure."

"Then, yes, I'll stay."

"Great. Good. I mean, we'd both better get to bed. Tomorrow's going to be crazy."

"I think whenever you have kids, crazy is the status quo."

Vancy started to rise, and though Matt knew he

should let her—just like he knew he should have let her leave when she suggested it—he wasn't ready to say good night. Being with her was addictive. He liked coming home and finding her in his house. He loved watching her with the boys.

Her every smile.

Her every laugh.

She sat back down, wrapped in his arm still, and all he could think of to say was her name. "Vancy."

Just that.

But in her name he wrapped so many things. None of which he could accurately identify, not even to himself. And because he couldn't define what he was feeling, he tried to tell her with a kiss. A simple touch of his lips to hers. At least that's what he told himself it would be. But the minute his lips met hers, he wanted more than just a touch . . . so much more.

And because he did, and because the rational side of his brain knew this was too soon for Vancy, who was still healing from her botched wedding and dealing with some very crazy situations, he backed off.

"Should I apologize?" he asked.

"If you did, then I'd have to apologize to you as well, because I'm pretty sure I was participating in that kiss."

"I didn't want to stop, but . . ."

"It's too soon for me," she filled in for him. "I

mean, I haven't totally reconciled myself to being dumped at the altar. And I definitely have to figure out why I'm not more torn up about losing Al. I planned to marry the man, and you'd think I'd be in agonizing pain right now. And there is some pain, but it's not agonizing by any stretch of the imagination. I'm embarrassed, I'm feeling harassed, but I'm not devastated, and you'd think I would be, wouldn't you?"

"I don't want to sound heartless, but maybe he did you a favor. Maybe, you two didn't—"

"Didn't have a real love? The kind you build a life and family on? You can say it, because, goodness knows, I've been thinking it. And if we didn't have that type of love, how could I have agreed to marry him? Because it was prudent? It was a good business decision? I have no idea." She stood. "You're right, it's too soon for this. I wouldn't want to use you."

"That's not what I meant." He stood too. "It's me who didn't want to use you. You're hurting, you're confused. We've both found ourselves in this absurd situation. We need to slow things down."

She nodded. "That's what Al said. Slow down, Vancy. That's why it took us three years to get engaged and another two years for the wedding that wasn't. You're right, this is way too fast." She turned and started toward the office. "Good night."

Matt sat back down on the couch. He'd been

right to slow things down. He knew it. She obviously knew it. Still, he felt a sense of loss. As if he'd somehow messed things up. He wasn't sure how, and he didn't know what to do about it, but he did know what he wanted to do. He wanted to go after her, pull her into his arms, and kiss her until all thoughts, all memories, of her ex were banished. He wanted to kiss her until all she could do was think about him.

And the fact that he did was why he really needed to stop. He hadn't been worried about Vancy's ex. The man lost any right to her when he left.

Matt's concern was with how very much he wanted her. They'd been acquaintances for years through her family. And he'd worked for her, designing her backyard redo. But they'd never been friends. They'd never even exchanged any words that didn't involve her backyard or his design.

And now they were kissing.

And he wanted to kiss her again.

He got up off the couch. This was getting him nowhere fast. He wasn't sure what was going on between them, and he wasn't going to figure it out tonight.

Chapter Seven

"Vancy! Vancy! Vancy!" the boys called the next day, though Vancy couldn't see them. It was an impromptu game of Marco Polo, without the pool or the proper words.

It had been raining all day, and she could sense the boys' energy was liable to burst out in an unpleasant way unless she found a way to release a bit of it. And Marcy and Don had both started to look a little frayed around the edges as the boys bopped from one end of the house to the other. So she'd suggested the game in Matt's rather barren basement.

"Vancy."

"Vancy."

"Vancy."

121

The boys had obviously split up to opposite sides of the long, damp room. Her sneakers made snapping sounds against the cement, and she could hear the boys' feet as well.

"Vancy."

She listened closely, finally pinpointed a set of footsteps, and moved in that direction, hands spread wide in case whichever boy it was tried to get around her.

Slowly she moved toward the noise.

"Vancy."

She could hear a muffled giggle.

"Vancy! Vancy!" one called from the opposite end of the room—trying to throw her off the scent, no doubt.

"Vancy!" She had to be close, because his voice had risen at least an octave.

"Vancy, watch out!"

Slam.

Since her arms were spread out, she hit whatever she hit with her face. Pain radiated like fine spokes being driven through her nose. She wondered if it had been driven into her brain. If the pain was any indication, it was likely.

"Ow."

She ripped off the blindfold.

"Oh, Vancy, you're bleeding!" Chris screamed.

"I don't like blood," Ricky said in a whisper,

then he leaned over and threw up onto the cement.

Vancy clutched her nose with one hand, trying to staunch the warm flow of blood.

"Grandpa! Grandpa!" Chris cried, running up the stairs for reinforcements.

"Vancy, I don't feel so good," Ricky said, looking up. His face turned even paler, and he leaned over and retched again.

Vancy ran to the washer and grabbed a towel she'd just folded that morning and pressed it to her aching nose, more to cover the sight of the blood than to stop the flow of it.

"Ricky, honey, I've covered it up, but don't look at me, just in case. Why don't you go upstairs, and I'll just clean up down here?"

"Okay, Vancy. Sorry."

"It's okay, buddy."

"It was a fun game, though."

"We'll do it again sometime." Although next time she'd make sure they played in the pool, since the current mishap had convinced her that Marco Polo was definitely an in-the-water-only game.

Ricky beat a retreat up the stairs, just as Don came to the top and yelled down, "Vancy, are you okay?"

"It's just a little nosebleed, and Ricky threw up. If you could go look after him, I'll clean up down here."

"You sure you're okay?"

"Positive."

She made short order of cleaning up both herself and Ricky's mess. After she finished, feeling more than a bit grimy, she went upstairs and took a quick shower. She was changing into fresh clothes when someone knocked on the bathroom door.

Matt's house was lovely, but, really, one and a half bathrooms made it a bit of a challenge with four adults and two kids crowded under his roof.

"I'll be right out," she called.

"Vancy, it's me."

She didn't need a name to know that the me in question was Matt. Her knees going slightly jiggly and her heart rate picking up its tempo were enough to tell her.

"Don't hurry," he continued. "I just got home and heard about the basement. Are you okay?"

"Fine. There's not even a mark on me. I'm more concerned about poor Ricky."

"He was in the kitchen eating ice cream with Chris, so I'm going to say he's made a total recovery."

"Good. I was worried."

"Anyway, you just take your time. Marcy and I are making dinner while Dad entertains the boys."

"You don't have to."

"Don't worry about it. I'm pretty sure it will involve takeout."

She laughed. "Great. Thanks."

Matt walked back down the hall, thankful to get away from the bathroom door. He couldn't seem to help but imagine what Vancy was wearing—or, rather, wasn't wearing—on the other side of the door. After their talk last night, he knew such thoughts were highly inappropriate.

Even without their talk those thoughts would be inappropriate.

But he just couldn't seem to stop himself.

He'd spent years bailing his brother out of one situation or another, but this one took the cake. He should be frazzled beyond belief and totally unable to think about anything but finding Mark and straightening out the boys' situation. Instead, his mind kept drifting to Vancy Salo.

It wasn't that he didn't care about the boys. He did. He wanted Mark to give him custody, to let him keep the boys here. He couldn't think of any better options for them, and, truth be told, it wasn't just them, it was him. He couldn't imagine the boys living anywhere but here.

And he couldn't imagine having the boys in his life and not having Vancy be a part of all their lives.

It wasn't that he wanted her as a babysitter. He

could hire someone. He was already in the process of looking for someone through a local agency.

No, it was more that they'd become a unit. Vancy, Ricky, Chris, and himself. They all fit together.

But was it fair to want her to stay?

He stepped out onto the enclosed back patio.

Sheltered from the rain, the boys and his father were busy building a clubhouse out of an old refrigerator box Matt had brought home. Given Chris and Ricky's affinity for tents, he thought it might entertain, and so far it was.

His dad poked his head out of a newly carved window. "How is she?"

"Fine. She'll be out soon."

"I remember once when you boys were little, I was trying to teach you the art of football, and I ended up practically eating the thing. Your brother, Mark, wasn't exactly a *marks*man."

"No, not exactly."

Chris and Ricky's heads poked out of the door to the clubhouse. "Will you teach us to play football, Grandpa?"

"I think that could be arranged."

Both boys were grinning as they popped back into the box.

"You all have fun. Let me go see if Marcy found my list of area restaurants that deliver."

"Marcy's not much of a cook, but she can order a meal with the best of them."

He went back into the kitchen and found Marcy and Vancy chatting like old friends.

"I invited Vancy's family over for an impromptu picnic tonight."

Vancy mouthed the word "Sorry" at him.

"I was talking with her grandmother, and she was saying everyone was worried about Vancy, since she's practically been in hiding since the aborted wedding, and I suggested that if Vancy won't go out and see them, then they should come here and see her. Dinner seemed like a logical solution. So they're all coming in a couple of hours. I've called Johnny-on-the-Square, and they're sending over an assortment of salads and rotisserie chickens. I do believe the rain is letting up, so we can all eat in the backyard, but we can make do on the patio if we must."

She rubbed her hands together as if brushing off crumbs from a difficult day in the kitchen. "Now I'm going to go check on Don and the boys."

She left the kitchen, and they both remained silent until they heard the patio door shut.

"Vancy, I'm sorry," Matt said at the same time she said, "I'm so sorry."

They laughed. And Matt shook his head. "She's a force to be reckoned with. A typhoon of sorts. And you know, even if the wind is trying to do a good thing, if it's that strong, it still blows you over."

Vancy laughed again, though it was a bit more nervous-sounding than before. "I have to warn you."

"Warn me?"

"Well, you've met Nana, and she's tough, but the rest of them . . . all together, all at once? Well, I love them, but they're a force of nature in and of themselves."

"I dealt with your grandmother all right."

"Yes, but if she's bringing Papa Bela—well, there's no dealing there. He's not going to be happy with this arrangement."

Matt felt confused, which was quickly becoming a feeling he knew intimately. "What arrangement?"

"My living with you."

"We can point out that you have an air mattress in the office, my father and stepmother in one room, and two little boys in a tent in the dining room."

"And he'll point out that you have a bedroom right next to the office."

"With all the people in the house, you can't sneeze anywhere that someone doesn't hear and bless you. How could he think anything was going on?"

"I'm not telling you it's right, or even logical, but I am telling you that Papa Bela is not going to be happy. Mom and Dad will probably be fine. They realize I'm an adult and tend to trust my judgment. My sister, Dori, won't just be fine, she'll think the whole thing is a great lark. But Papa Bela and my brother, Noah, are not going to listen to logic."

Matt grinned, though he wasn't sure why. "So what you're saying is that this is going to be an interesting dinner?"

"I do believe that's an understatement if ever I heard one."

Vancy was trying to smile convincingly, but Matt could tell it was forced. "It's going to be fine, Vancy. I'm a big boy. I can handle your grandfather and your brother."

She snorted, and Matt felt more than a bit insulted. "You don't think so?"

"One-on-one, no problem, but the whole Salo clan? Even Marcy couldn't handle them."

"You've got to relax. It'll be fine."

"I don't know if I can. I've got this sick feeling in the pit of my stomach, and it has nothing to do with whacking myself on that support beam in the basement."

"Oh, about that, come here." He pulled her close and examined her. "I don't think you're going to have any permanent scars." His hand gently brushed her nose. "No, it looks fine to me."

Vancy swallowed hard. "Uh, that's good. I'd hate to have a Cyrano nose."

"There's something I've learned a lot about this past week, and I meant to do it right away."

"What's that?"

"Kiss your boo-boo and make it better." He nodded. "Yes, I have it on good authority that boo-boos can't heal properly without a kiss."

"You don't have to—"

"I know, but maybe I want to." He leaned in and placed a featherlight kiss on her forehead, followed by one on her nose. "There. All better?"

Vancy smiled. "Well, you did miss a couple spots."

Matt hadn't realized he was holding his breath until he let it out with a whoosh. He felt as if he were grinning so broadly, his face was in danger of splitting. "Do tell, Ms. Salo. I'd hate to have it said that I run a haphazard operation here. Just where did I miss?"

She touched her lips. "If you don't mind."

"I think I can manage it." He leaned forward, and the kiss was as sweet as the others they'd shared. It had barely started when . . .

"Grandpa, Grandpa! Ricky! Come in here! Uncle Matt's kissin' Vancy!"

Vancy pulled back from Matt as if burned by fire. "Your uncle was just kissing my boo-boo."

"Oh, like he did when Ricky fell?"

"Just like that."

"He was kissing you longer, and he wasn't kissin' your nose."

"What happened?" Don asked, Ricky right behind him.

"Uncle Matt was kissin' Vancy's boo-boo, but his lips slipped from her nose to her mouth."

"Did they now?" Don asked, looking highly amused.

"Yeah, and he was kissin' Vancy lots longer than he kissed your boo-boo, Ricky."

"Hey, Uncle Matt, how come you kissed Vancy longer?"

"I didn't. It was just a little peck—"

Marcy walked in. "What's all the commotion?"

"Uncle Matt was kissing Vancy's boo-boo," Ricky said, filling her in.

"Only he forgot it was on her nose," Chris added.

"Or he slipped."

"And kissed her lips instead."

As if a thought occurred to them both at the same moment, they said in unison, "Ew. Girl germs."

"Why do I feel like I'm back in grade school, and kids are chanting, 'Vancy's got the cooties'?"

"What's cooties?" Ricky asked with apparent interest.

"Yeah, what?"

"Like girl germs but worse," Matt said oh, so helpfully.

"Oh, Vancy's got the cooties!" the boys chanted together.

"Maybe I don't have the cooties. Maybe your Uncle Matt does," she tried.

"Yeah, Uncle Matt has the cooties!" the twins singsonged together.

"Uh, boys, maybe we should go back to finish your clubhouse. It sounds like Nana Vancy's coming over and bringing more of Vancy's family."

"Hey, Vancy, do they all tell cool stories like you and Nana do, 'cause you guys tell the coolest."

Even at five, Chris had the good sense to realize what he'd said, and he quickly added, "And Grandma Marcy does too."

"Grandma," Marcy whispered, and Matt could have sworn there were tears in her eyes. "Well, Grandma Marcy"—she repeated the words as if savoring the sound—"might not tell the best stories, but she does order the best dinners around. Guess what they're bringing us for dessert?"

"What?"

"Chocolate cake and ice cream."

With the boys screaming their appreciation of the night's menu, his dad and Marcy led them back outside to finish the cardboard clubhouse.

Matt just watched them go, feeling thunderstruck. "I never really disliked Marcy, but I'll admit, I didn't really try to get to know her. I'm sorry about that now. Did you see how she reacted . . ."

He turned to look at Vancy, who had tears welling in her eyes. "Yes, I saw. She was so thrilled. Some people just aren't good at expressing their feelings. I've seen her look at your dad, watched her while she talks about him. She loves him. Pure and simple. Just loves him."

"And for that alone, I owe her." He paused. "Now, where were we?"

"We were going to go see if we can pick up the toys in the living room before we get inundated by Salos."

"I was thinking about . . ." He just grinned.

She smiled shyly back at him. "I know what you were thinking, but there's a time and place for everything, and this is neither the time, nor the place to share our cooties."

"You sound like my old English teacher."

"Good. Maybe you'll be able to concentrate on something other than kissing."

"No, it's not so good. My English teacher was hot. It was her first year out of college."

"Sheesh. Toys, Matt. We're picking up toys."

"I think my idea's better."

She laughed as she walked into the living room, and the sound delighted Matt as much as the kiss had. Well, that was a lie. It delighted him *almost* as much as the kiss had.

"Maybe later, after we pick up the toys, I can get a kiss?"

She laughed again. "Maybe."

"Da-da-da-da." Vancy whispered the theme to *Jaws* as a line of her family's cars pulled into

Matt's drive, like some Gypsy caravan. First Nana Vancy and Papa Bela, then her mom and dad, with Dori in their car, and finally Noah and his fiancée, Julianna.

"Come on, it's not going to be that bad," Matt said, sounding completely confident in his assessment.

Vancy turned around and shot him a look. She watched as his confidence withered.

"Is it?" he asked, sounding unsure now.

"I love my family" was her reply. That was the truth. She did love her family, but a full-out Salo get-together used to have Al searching for any and every excuse he could find to get out of it. It wasn't that he didn't like her family, he was always quick to assure her. It was simply that he liked her family better in small doses.

Vancy knew Matt liked her grandmother but worried that all the Salos at once would prove to be too big a dose for him to handle.

As if sensing her nervousness, he took her hand in his and gave it a squeeze. "It's fine."

"Oh, they're here," Marcy said as she entered the room and saw the line of cars. "Now, don't just stand there, you two. I know you have better manners than that. Open the door and let them in."

Vancy and Matt moved in unison toward the front door, and both seemed to realize at the same moment that they were still holding hands. They both let go at the same time.

Vancy looked up and felt her face warm. "Sorry."

Matt frowned, then simply nodded. She wasn't sure if his expression had to do with finding himself holding her hand, or with her apology, but she didn't have time to ask.

He opened the door. "Mrs. Salo," he said by way of greeting.

"Nana," her grandmother scolded. "You just call me Nana like everyone else. Come in, everyone. That way we'll just make the introductions once." She kissed Matt's cheek, then spied Vancy and kissed hers as well.

"Don, bring the boys in. Our guests have arrived!" Marcy bellowed.

Everyone filed in, the two families lining opposite sides of the entryway.

Vancy rarely thought about the height of her grandfather, father, and brother, but, standing next to Matt, it struck her that they really were large men. They were all a good three or more inches taller than Matt and his dad. It was apparent, but not nearly as stark a difference as between the three of them and Al, who'd barely brushed five eleven.

"Okay, I'll do my family. Matt, you do yours. This is my grandfather, Bela."

"Papa," Nana said to Matt and the boys. "Come here, boys." They ran over, and both hugged her. "This is Chris, and this is Ricky. Two of the most special boys in the world."

The boys looked at Vancy's grandmother and simply beamed.

"So, Nana, Papa, and this is my father and mother, Emil and Mary Jane, my brother, Noah, his fiancée, Julianna, and my baby sister, Dori."

"My father, Don, my stepmother, Marcy, and Nana took care of introducing you to my nephews, Rick and Chris."

"Let's get this dinner started." Nana came up to Marcy. "I know you ordered in, but I'd already started a pot of my chicken paprikash, so I brought it along. I hope you don't mind."

"Is it a Hungarian dish?"

Nana nodded. "My mother used to make it for me. I use real Hungarian paprika. I've tried the kind in the grocery stores here, but it's just not the same. I have a cousin's daughter who sends me shipments from home. Now, that's how paprika should taste. I remember when I was little, my mother used to have strings of garlic and her peppers on the shed's wall. The wall was white, and it made the colors really stand out."

"I can't wait to sample it. I don't know if I'd ever tried Hungarian cuisine before," Marcy was saying as the two of them made their way toward the kitchen.

Vancy turned back and saw her father, grandfather, and brother standing too close to Matt, just staring at him without saying anything.

"So, you're living with my daughter," her father finally said.

"No, sir. I mean, yes, sir, but not like that. I—"

Vancy cut off his explanation. "I'm sleeping on my air mattress in Matt's office, he's in his room, Don and Marcy are in the spare room, and the boys have been making a tent each night. I will point out that I'm telling you this as a courtesy, not because I think it's truly any of your business. I'm an adult, remember?"

"Your mother said you're on the rebound and don't know what you're doing," her father said stubbornly, still glaring at Matt.

"Dad, name me a situation, a specific situation, where you felt I didn't know what I was doing."

"Al," her brother, Noah, said helpfully.

"That doesn't count." She glared at him.

"That's it." Nana appeared in the doorway like magic. "I call a truce. Matt was a hero, taking our Vancy away from the media. They've stalked all of us, especially me, so I'm more sympathetic than you men. Matt, he really did save the day, and we owe him our thanks, not an inquisition."

"And may I point out," her mother said, "that all of us liked Al. None of us saw anything wrong, so if there's any fault, it's not in Vancy's judgment, it's a Salo family fault."

"So stop being the testosterone trio and leave Matt alone." Dori, who was almost as tall as Matt, crowded in between him and the Salo men. "Down, boys."

"Yes," her mom said, elbowing her way into the crowd. "All of you go out back, and we'll go help Matt's stepmother and Nana get the dinner together."

"But—" her father started, but at one look from her mom, he shut up and followed Matt toward the back patio door.

"I'll go with the guys and maintain order," Dori said.

Vancy just laughed, letting Dori know she knew the real reason her sister was heading out back. Dori had grown up a tomboy, and becoming an adult hadn't changed that a bit. She still would rather be outdoors with the men than indoors with the women any day of the week.

"I'll help," Julianna said. As always, in a family get-together situation, Julianna just seemed to fade into the woodwork. They all tried to include her, make her feel like part of the family, but Vancy always had the feeling that it wasn't quite working.

Julianna's sister, Cassie, on the other hand,

worked for the company and always felt more like family than an employee or friend. It worried Vancy. She didn't know how to reach this elusive, soon to be sister-in-law.

"Good," Vancy said.

"Now, tell us about Matt's nephews," her mother instructed. "Your grandmother wouldn't say where you were, so we didn't know anything about any of them until Matt's stepmother called and invited us for dinner."

"I just need some time and—"

"Space," her mother filled in. She wrapped her arms around Vancy. "Sweetheart, I do understand. Truly. And I'm glad you're feeling better. It will take time to get over Al, but . . ."

That was the problem, Vancy thought as her mother went on trying to comfort her. It wasn't going to take time to get over Al. She was pretty sure she was already quite over him.

Oh, the being-left-at-the-altar part was still embarrassing, and she wasn't going to enjoy the monumental task of returning all the wedding gifts, but she didn't miss Al at all.

". . . we're all here for you."

"I know you are, Mom."

"Okay, let's stop this lollygagging and get to feeding the crowd out back," Nana Vancy, aka the general, said.

If Nana was the general, then Marcy was a

four-star version, because she began calling out orders that sent the rest of them scurrying and that had the picnic table set in short order.

Vancy had worried that the dinner would be uncomfortable but was delighted to discover it was anything but. Matt, though he wasn't in contracting, was in a closely related field, which meant he fit right in with the family, and they all discussed the current local housing trends.

When her mother, who could take only so much shoptalk, she proclaimed, changed topics, a rousing discussion of the boys, of preschools in the area, and kids in general commenced. Noah suggested that every child needed a swing set, and from there it was decided that not just any traditional swing set would do, and pretty soon everyone had a sheet of paper and all of them were excitedly sketching plans for a play palace. Swing, clubhouse, teeter-totter, sandbox—everything two small boys could want.

Vancy sat back and listened and was struck by how easily Matt fit in with her family. Al never had. Julianna never had. She'd thought it was her family that was the problem, but seeing Matt fit right in, she wondered if it had been Al, and not some familial flaw.

Watching them all argue the merits of wood chips versus other cushioning floorings for the play area, she decided not to analyze it too hard.

She made up her mind to just sit back and enjoy the evening.

When dinner was finished, Marcy cleared her throat.

"Marcy?" Vancy asked. Marcy shook her head, looked from Don to Matt, and cleared her throat again. It sounded rather like she was a cat with a hair ball.

Don finally looked up. "Yes, dear?"

"These dishes won't clear themselves. I think anyone who rushed to the backyard when it was time to set the table should clear. Don't you, Don?" She gave him a look that had him jumping to his feet.

"Why, I was just going to suggest it, dear." Matt's dad started picking up plates.

When no one else followed suit, Marcy cleared her throat again as she looked from one man to the next, and finally her gaze landed on Dori.

It had a cattle-prod-like effect, and all of them jumped to their feet and started clearing.

"Wow," Vancy said, as even Dori, who, to the best of Vancy's knowledge, hadn't cleared a table without kicking and screaming ever, left with the remains of the meal. "That was amazing, Marcy."

"Everyone has talents, Vancy, and prodding people into doing the right thing is one of mine." Marcy looked quite pleased with herself without looking out-and-out smug.

When the clearing crew returned, they brought everyone another round of drinks, and Matt brought a bag of marshmallows. They built a fire in his fire pit, and soon everyone was roasting marshmallows and talking. The boys moved from lap to lap, basking in the adult attention.

Finally, after the sun went down, Noah and Matt taught the boys the art of catching fireflies.

As Vancy's family packed up to go home, the boys were hugged by one and all.

"Night, Nana. Night . . ." They hesitated over what to call her grandfather.

"I'm your Papa Bela, boys. If your uncle says it's okay, I'll take you out fishing sometime soon. I taught all my kids and grandkids to fish. Would you like that?"

The boys' heads bobbled enthusiastically.

"Matt?" Papa Bela asked.

"That would be fine, sir."

"And, Don, if you're still in town, we'd love to have you along."

"If not this trip, I'll take a rain check for the next time I'm in Erie."

The two men shook hands, as if sealing a deal.

After they'd gotten Vancy's family all out the door, Marcy dragged Don into the kitchen to finish tidying up, and Vancy and Matt tag-teamed the boys into a bath and then pajamas.

As they tucked them in, Chris asked, "Vancy,

could you tell us about fishing with Papa Bela for a bedtime story?"

She smiled and regaled them with the story of her grandfather's nemesis, Gilbert the Bluegill. That her grandmother used to say Gilbert had to be magic, because there was no way he could have escaped Bela so many times otherwise. That Nana said if anyone ever did catch the fish, he'd probably be worth at least a wish or two.

"Maybe we'll catch 'im," Ricky said sleepily.

"What would you wish?" Vancy asked, looking at the two sleepyheads in the tent.

"I'd wish to always live with you and Uncle Matt."

"Yeah," Chris echoed.

Vancy didn't know what to say to that, so she simply leaned over and kissed the twin foreheads and closed the flap of the makeshift tent under the dining room table.

They walked out of the dining room, and Matt started, "About their wish—"

Marcy and Don came out of the kitchen. "Well, that was a lot of fun, Vancy. Your family is delightful." Marcy smiled.

"I think so too, but I'm glad you agree. And I have to thank you for putting it all together. It was a lovely evening."

"Yeah," Matt added, and he kissed his stepmother's cheek.

She blushed and took Don's hand. "Come on, sweetie. It's time for bed."

Matt followed Vancy down the hall to the office door. "Well, this is where we say good night."

Vancy just nodded, though she didn't make any move to open the office door.

"I like your family." Matt's voice was soft.

Vancy had a sudden urge to rest her cheek against his chest and see if it vibrated as he spoke. Instead, she stood her ground and said, "I like my family too." She paused, then added, "Well, most of the time."

They both laughed, then stood in silence. Vancy wasn't sure, but she thought Matt was going to kiss her again. And she wasn't sure she should let him, but she was very sure she wanted to. "The boys will still probably get up at the crack of dawn."

Matt nodded. "Yes, probably."

"And you have that early meeting."

"Yes."

"So, we should say good night."

He nodded and leaned down and kissed her forehead. "Night, Vancy."

Talk about disappointing.

A chaste kiss on the forehead was worse than no kiss at all. Because if he hadn't kissed her, she could imagine it simply hadn't occurred to him, but that brisk brush of his lips on her forehead said he did think of it and opted not. Oh, he was being a gentleman—she knew that—but she didn't want a gentleman. She wanted . . .

And she reached up, placing her hands gently behind his neck and standing on tiptoe until she could reach his lips. Then she kissed him good night in a way that bore no resemblance to his platonic forehead-kiss of a moment ago.

"Well . . ." was all he said. A slow grin spread across his face.

"Yes, well." She smiled back.

His smile dimmed a bit. "We should probably talk about this."

She shook her head. She didn't want to spoil the moment by analyzing it. "Not tonight. Tonight I'm going to sleep."

He looked as if he was going to argue, but instead he simply nodded and went next door to his bedroom.

Vancy went into her makeshift office-bedroom and was under the covers in short order. But sleep didn't come nearly as fast. As a matter of fact, she tossed and turned for the longest time, and when she finally did doze off, she dreamed about her wedding.

She was walking down the aisle in her wedding dress, her heart beating far too fast, her breath coming in short bursts. She couldn't see her groom at the front of the church, and she felt a wave of sadness. He wasn't coming.

But then a shadowy figure in a tux appeared like magic. She breathed a sigh of relief and studied the figure, straining to see his face and reassure herself it was indeed he.

She realized her dad was at her side. "It'll be all right now, honey," he whispered.

She turned and smiled at him, then looked back at the faceless tuxedoed groom and realized she could indeed see his face.

It wasn't Al.

It was Matt.

And she cried out with happiness. The sound in her dream woke her up with a start, and she wondered if she'd cried out for real. But when no one else in the house made any noise, she figured she hadn't and flopped back onto the pillow.

Vancy wasn't sure what she felt about the dream, and she refused to analyze it. Instead, she turned on her iPod and fell asleep to the sounds of Broadway's *Wicked*.

Chapter Eight

Nancy spent the rest of the week not analyzing what was going on between Matt and herself. She didn't analyze it when they sat side by side on the couch watching TV after the boys were in bed.

She didn't analyze it when she caught him smiling at her as she read the boys a story.

She didn't analyze it when his father and Marcy said good-bye and promised to be back in a week or so to visit, and she realized she wouldn't be sleeping in the office on her air mattress anymore when they came back.

And she absolutely didn't analyze it when she kissed Matt.

And they kissed an awful lot.

With so many people in the house, even stealing

a kiss could be tricky, but they managed it, laughing like kids.

In addition to not analyzing, they didn't mention her going home on Friday, and they certainly didn't mention Matt's brother, Mark, and the potential custody issue.

The lawyer in Vancy knew they should.

But the woman in Vancy didn't want to spoil this sweet interlude. Soon enough Friday would arrive, and she'd have to pack up her clothes and her air mattress, and Matt and the boys would take her home. That following Monday she'd go to work and fall right back into her normal routine.

As long as she wasn't analyzing, Vancy didn't analyze why the thought of going back to her old life left her feeling sort of cold and hollow.

Thursday night, she tucked the boys into bed.

"Vancy," Ricky said, reaching up and hugging her. "I love you."

Chris, not to be left out, stood up and wrapped his arms around her neck as well. "I love you too."

"Me and Ricky want you to be our mommy."

"Yeah."

A huge lump formed in Vancy's throat, and she sat on the bed and pulled both boys onto her lap. "Boys, you already have a mom."

"Nuh-uh." Ricky shook his head. "She's gone. She left us with the mean grandma, but then we came to stay with Uncle Matt and you. We wanna stay here with you, and you can be our mom."

"Remember we talked about this? I don't live here. I just stayed with Uncle Matt to help him, but tomorrow it's time for me to go home. Uncle Matt's found a wonderful day care center that you'll go to when he's at work."

He'd come home with the brochure yesterday. Outings, swimming, games, and friends. It looked lovely and allowed him a lot of flexibility. He sounded pleased with it, and Vancy had tried to be as happy about it, but she wasn't sure how well that was going. And as both boys started crying, something in Vancy broke. She felt tears gather in her eyes as well.

She realized she wasn't any happier about leaving than they were, and though the day care center might have a wonderful program, she hated the idea as much as the boys appeared to.

She knew she had to put on an excited face, so she blinked back her tears and tried to stretch her lips into a smile. "Just think of all the new friends you'll make—kids your own age to play with."

"We don't want new friends," Chris said, with a hiccup for emphasis. "We want you to be our mom."

"And stay here with us and Uncle Matt and never leave." Ricky wiped his nose on his pajama sleeve for emphasis.

"Boys, I wish I could stay and never leave." As she said the words, she realized it wasn't just the boys she wanted to stay with. It was Matt. They'd built this impromptu family, and she wanted to keep it.

No, she wasn't being entirely honest with herself.

She had grown to love the boys, but her feelings for Matt were independent of Chris and Ricky. She . . . cared for him.

No, that was too shallow a description.

She loved him.

The realization hit her hard. Looking at the boys' teary eyes, she knew she had to push the new, wonderful feeling aside and concentrate on them.

She leaned down and kissed their foreheads in turn. "Boys, I wish I could stay here forever, but I have a house of my own. I have a job. I took time off, but now I have to go back." She felt no sense of anticipation about getting back to work. For years work had been the driving force in her life, but suddenly it didn't seem as important. But, as she'd told the boys, she had to go back.

"Listen, I can't be your mom, and I might not live with you and your Uncle Matt, but that doesn't mean I don't love you. I'll always love you, and nothing can change that."

"But you won't live here," Chris maintained.

"No, I won't, but you can come visit my house, and I'll come visit you both all the time."

Ricky whispered, "What if our real mom comes to take us away?" She heard the fear in the question.

"Or our real dad comes?" Chris added. "We don't want to leave Uncle Matt."

Part of Vancy wanted to promise them that that would never happen, that she wouldn't let it, but she knew that the law placed a lot of emphasis on a biological parent's rights. She wouldn't lie to the boys.

"If your mom comes back, or your dad comes, I can't promise what will happen, but I can promise that your uncle will do all that he can to make sure you're both somewhere that you can be happy, and I promise I'll help him."

"And you'll still love us?" Ricky asked.

She drew them both into a hug, her head sandwiched between theirs. "No matter where I am, or where you both are, I will love you. Nothing in the whole world can change that. You see, I love you more than . . ." She searched for something the boys could relate to. "More than pizza."

Ricky caught on first. "More than ice cream?"

Vancy nodded, and Ricky smiled a wisp of a smile.

"More than chocolate," she added.

Chris was smiling now as well. "How 'bout more than birthday cake?"

Vancy nodded her head solemnly and promised, "More than a hundred birthday cakes and presents."

Both boys looked suitably impressed as she hugged them again.

She might be caught in a whirlwind of change and emotions, she might not have sorted any of it out, but this required no sorting, no thought. Her love for the boys just was. "I promise, I will always love you both."

"And you'll come to visit and tell us more Nana Vancy stories?" Ricky checked.

Vancy laughed. "You bet. And I bet Nana Vancy will come over as well and tell you some herself."

"We love Nana Vancy."

Still feeling choked up, Vancy managed, "She loves you both too. We all do." Then, turning all-business before she totally lost control of her emotions, she said, "Okay, now snuggle in, and I'll tell you a Nana Vancy story."

She disentangled herself from them with reluctance and tucked them both into the bed, then sat on the edge and started, "Once upon a time, in—"

"Hungary," the boys supplied in unison.

She nodded. "In Hungary, a land of magic and beauty, there lived a young girl named Vancy. One day she went into the woods near her house. . . ."

Matt stood in the doorway, listening to Vancy weave her story-spell around the boys, and something in his heart constricted. For so many years he'd lived here alone. He'd wanted it that way. He'd wanted to focus on his business. And he had. Everything Wilde was a success.

So now what?

He'd had relationships, but they'd only been passing fancies, no one he really missed when they'd ended. But he'd miss Vancy, and the hell of it was, he wasn't sure if what they had even counted as a relationship. A friendship punctuated by a few kisses, maybe.

He listened to her story weaving the boys a picture of love, of family. The boys laughed, and Vancy joined them, their three voices harmonizing.

Matt realized that suddenly his empty house was filled with people and laughter. Because of the boys.

Because of Vancy.

He hated the thought of her leaving tomorrow as much as the boys did. He wanted her to stay. And the reason wasn't that she was good to and for the boys, though that was part of it.

It wasn't that he was worried that the press would still bother her, though that was a part of it as well.

It was that he cared about her.

No, that was a cop-out. As he watched her hug the boys and kiss their foreheads, he realized it was much more than caring.

He loved her.

It was fast.

Probably too fast.

But there was no denying the feeling. He loved her. He couldn't imagine what their lives would be without her here.

She got up from the bed and turned, spotted him, and smiled. "Did you come to say good night?"

He nodded mutely, afraid to trust his voice.

He moved to the bed, hugged both boys, and managed to say, "Night, guys. See you in the morning."

He flipped off the light and the Mickey Mouse night-light automatically blinked on. It was just one of the things Vancy had thought to buy that first night on their shopping spree. It glowed warmly.

He walked out of the room and shut the door all but a crack.

"Thanks for letting me tuck them in myself tonight, since it's my last night."

"About that . . ." He was going to do it. He was going to tell her that he loved her, that he knew it was too soon, that he knew she was still hurting about losing her fiancé but that he hoped she'd give him a chance, continue to see him, and give her own feelings a chance to grow. "I wanted . . . no, I need to say—"

The doorbell rang.

Matt wanted to growl with frustration but settled

for saying, "Hold that thought." He wondered who it was and how fast he could get rid of them.

"What thought?" Vancy asked, obviously curious.

She followed on his heels as he went to the front door and opened it, ready to brush off whoever was there.

No brush-off came to mind as he saw who their late-night visitor was. "Mark."

Leave it to his brother to show up and ruin what he hoped was going to be a good moment.

Mark stepped into the house, tossed a small overnight bag onto the floor, then spied Vancy. Matt didn't need to turn around to know she was there behind him.

Mark grinned and gave him a slap on the shoulder. "Oh, you've got a woman here. Nice. And here I was thinking you were married to your business."

Matt tried to reign in his anger. His brother was here, laughing and joking around, as if he didn't have a care in the world. As if he didn't have two sons he'd never acknowledged or worried about. "Come in. We need to talk."

Vancy turned and headed for the kitchen. "I'll just leave you two to your talk."

"Vancy, stop," Matt said, just as Mark said, "Aren't you going to introduce us?"

Mark didn't wait for Matt to respond, he just stuck out his hand and said, "Mark Wilde."

Vancy took it with marked reluctance. "Vancy Salo. And now I'll be going."

"Oh, I'd rather you stayed." Mark shot her a look that Matt readily recognized. It was the suave look that generally drew women right into Mark's arms.

Vancy's expression simply hardened. "No, I—"

Matt took her hand. "It's fine with me, Vancy. After all, you already have a pretty good handle on the situation."

"But I—" She stopped and looked at Matt, as if she could read his expression. She gave him a small smile and nodded her head.

"See? We insist." Mark walked into the living room as if he owned it. "You can sit by me." He went to the love seat and patted the cushion next to him.

"I think I'd rather sit over here." She moved to the couch, and Matt followed her.

Matt was furious with his brother, but rather than yelling at him, he tread softly, trying to remember that the ultimate goal was Mark's giving him custody of the boys. "Mark, I've been trying to reach you."

"I know. I got your messages. Is something wrong with Dad?" There was genuine concern on his face.

"No, not Dad. It's your sons."

"My what?" Mark froze, and a deer-in-the-headlights expression flashed across his face, quickly replaced by a confused look.

Matt wasn't buying it. "Your looking confused would probably convince anyone else, but not me."

"Fine." Belligerence screamed in the way Mark held his body, as if daring anyone to call him on the carpet. "How'd you find out?"

"The question is, how could you just leave them like that?" Matt asked softly.

"Hey, I couldn't be sure they were mine, and I gave their mother money. Cleaned out my bank account, if I recall correctly."

"Mark." Matt had thought he'd long since become immune to Mark, but listening to his brother now, he knew he could still be hurt. "I don't understand you."

"I don't need this." He pushed up off the love seat, as if he planned on leaving.

Matt jumped to his feet, blocking his brother's exit. "Mark, you need to stay until at least tomorrow, so we can straighten this out."

"Straighten what out?"

"The boys' mother left them with a grandmother to bring to you. She brought them to me instead."

"Left them?"

"There was a letter. I read it." He didn't feel a bit guilty about it. "She didn't want custody. She said she'd done her share, and now it was your turn. She sent papers to that effect."

"But I don't want . . ." His sentence faded away, and he stood there looking defensive. But underneath that was something more. Maybe fear?

"Mark, if you tell me you want to make a go of it, I'll back you one hundred percent." It cost him to say the words, but he couldn't just dismiss his brother's choice in the matter.

Mark shook his head. "Me, a father? I never planned on going that route. I don't want to be tied down."

Hearing Mark say the words left Matt feeling both relieved and sorry . . . sorry that his brother could so easily dismiss Chris and Rick as an inconvenience. "You might not want, but I do. So stay until tomorrow, we'll go to a lawyer, and you can give me legal guardianship of the boys. Then you can go back to whatever you were doing."

"That's all?" Mark asked, clearly suspicious. "No recriminations, no telling me I need to step up and take responsibility?"

"This isn't some job that you can just try on and discard, that if you walk away, there's no one hurt but you. This is about two little boys, and, no, I'm not going to tell you to step up and take responsibility for them, because you can't even take care of yourself."

"I'm not going to apologize for the way I live my life. And I'm smart enough to realize that two little boys wouldn't fit in."

There it was again, that hint of something in Mark's expression. Maybe it wasn't fear. Maybe it was wistfulness?

"Mark, I mean it, if you told me you honestly wanted to be with them, to do right by them, you could stay here, and I'd help—"

His brother just shook his head. "Don't get your panties in a wad, Matt. I might not be much of a father, but I'm good enough to realize they're better off without me."

"If you'd just try to change, you could—"

"Don't you see? I don't want to change. I never tried to change for you or for Dad, and I'm certainly not going to do it for two kids I've never known."

Maybe, with time, Mark would grow up, but he was right. He couldn't do it for any of them; he'd have to do it for himself. After years of trying, Matt knew he couldn't force his brother, so all he could do was wait and hope. And see to it that the boys were cared for and loved.

"But you'll stay?" he pressed. "I just want to be sure everything's as legal as I can get it."

Mark nodded. "I'll stay until tomorrow, but then I'm out of here."

"Mark—"

His brother cut him off. "So, where am I sleeping?"

"The house is a bit crowded. You can have the couch."

"Fine." He got up off the love seat and started unbuttoning his top. "I'm stripping for bed. So, princess, if you don't want a show, you'd best go."

Vancy, still silent, hurried into the hall, and Matt followed closely behind her.

"I'm sorry" was all he could think of to say.

She looked surprised. "For what?"

"For that."

"You've done nothing but be an upstanding man. When you offered to help Mark if he wanted the boys . . ." Vancy wanted to say that when he made that offer, she'd known, beyond any shadow of a doubt, beyond any worries about rebounds or ex-fiancés, that she loved him.

She'd fallen in love with the boys practically at first sight, and so it didn't seem odd that she'd fallen for their uncle just as hard and fast.

She didn't say any of it, though. Matt had enough on his plate right now, and she'd bide her time, but she'd tell him soon. For now she settled with saying, "Matt, you are an amazing man who has nothing to be sorry for."

"Amazing?" He grinned, as if taking her words as a joke.

Not ready to outline her feelings for him, she settled for trying to tell him with a kiss. She stood on tiptoe, wrapped her arms around his neck, and tried to put all her new and powerful emotions into a brief touch of her lips to his.

Regretfully, she broke off and took a step back. Before any of the words that seemed pressing to come out could escape her tight control, she asked, "May I use your computer before I go to bed?"

Her abrupt change of subject left Matt looking confused. "Uh, sure."

She took another step back, wanting to put distance between herself and her almost physical need to touch him. "Thanks. I'll get started on having an agreement drawn up, so that we can get all the details squared away first thing. I don't know that I'd want to chance . . ." She let the sentence trail off, because there was no way to say that she didn't want to chance Mark's changing his mind and not sound rude.

"It's okay," Matt said, sadness in his voice. "I know how Mark is. Knowing doesn't mean I don't keep hoping he'll change, but I do understand what he's like, even though I'll never really understand him."

She leaned up and kissed his cheek. "You're a good man, Matt Wilde."

She hurried into his office, her makeshift bedroom, and turned on the computer. Thinking about a legal document was ever so much easier than thinking about her newly untangled emotions.

After all, now that she'd admitted to herself that she loved Matt, she was left with the task of telling him about her feelings. And though he seemed to enjoy kissing her, seemed to genuinely like her, she'd had no indication that his feelings went any deeper.

When Al walked away, she'd been embarrassed and hurt, but it was nothing like the pain she knew she'd feel if Matt turned away from her.

She pushed her worries aside and started working on a custody agreement.

Chapter Nine

I t was too quiet.

That was Vancy's first thought as she lifted her head from Matt's desk, where she'd obviously spent the night. She sat up and twisted and turned, trying to work out the huge crick in her neck she'd acquired as a result of her inadvertent choice of bed.

She jiggled the mouse, and the computer screen woke back up as well, revealing a draft of a custody agreement. She attached it to an e-mail and sent it off to Jarrad at the firm. He'd had more experience in this kind of thing, and she'd welcome his input. She wanted to be sure all the *t*'s were crossed and all the *i*'s were dotted.

Vancy stood and realized it wasn't just her neck that was stiff—her legs felt as if they had ten-pound weights attached to them. She blinked rapidly, trying to clear the grit from her eyes.

She hadn't pulled an all-nighter like this since college. She glanced at the clock.

Eight-thirty?

She couldn't remember the last time she'd woken up so late. She listened but heard nothing. The silence was what worried her.

She hurried down the hall to check on the boys, but their bed was empty. Wondering if she'd put all the vinegar and baking soda up out of reach, she moved quietly down the hall and found them sitting on the floor in front of the couch, staring at Mark, who was still sleeping there, sprawled on his back, one leg hanging off and onto the floor.

"He looks like Uncle Matt," Chris stage-whispered to Rick.

"Boys, come on," Vancy called softly, trying to get them into the kitchen. The boys didn't move. She couldn't tell if they hadn't heard her or were ignoring her. They just continued kneeling by the sleeping man, studying him.

"He's not Uncle Matt, though, is he, Vancy?" Ricky asked, turning to look at her and confirming that they'd indeed been ignoring her. She didn't have time to formulate an answer before he added, "He's our dad, right?"

Mark's eyes snapped open, and he spotted the boys and jumped. "What the h—" He cut himself off, pulled the covers up to his chin, and glared at the boys.

Chris and Rick weren't so easily intimidated. Remembering the quiet, reserved boys she'd met that first night, Vancy liked to think that their new confidence was due to the fact that they felt safe here.

"You're our dad, right?" Rick asked.

Mark just studied them and shrugged. "Maybe."

"Did you come to take us with you?" Chris didn't look pleased at the prospect. "'Cause if you did, we'll run away." He stood, as if ready to run right that second.

"Yeah." Ricky stood as well. "We don't want to go with you."

"You look like Uncle Matt, but you're not him. We want to live here with him and Vancy. And our grandma and grandpa are going to come back and take us fishing and to Waldemeer—they've got waterslides there—and Nana Vancy will tell us stories and make us cookies."

"Yeah."

Their bravado finally wore off, and they ran to Vancy, wrapping their arms around her legs. "Don't let him take us away, Vancy. We want to stay here. We'll be good. We'll pick up, and we'll go to bed whenever you say."

"We'll even take naps," Chris added.

She disentangled their arms from her legs and

knelt down. "Boys, let's start this all over again. This is your father, Mark. Mark, this is Chris and Rick. Boys, your father thought you were with your mom and just found out you weren't, so he hurried here to make sure you were okay, didn't you, Mark?"

Still looking confused and half asleep, Mark just nodded.

"Your Uncle Matt and I talked to your father last night, and he's agreed that you should stay here. He doesn't have a house, and he knows you're happy here with Uncle Matt, so he's going to sign some papers today saying you can stay with Uncle Matt."

"He won't take us away?" Ricky asked, peeking around at Mark.

"No," Mark said, finding his voice. "No, I promise I won't."

"But maybe"—Vancy looked over the boys' dark heads, her eyes meeting Mark's—"he'll stay a day or two so you can get to know him, then he could call and come visit. Wouldn't that be nice?"

Chris turned and eyed Mark suspiciously, then turned back to Vancy. "But he won't take us?"

"No. No one is going to take you from your Uncle Matt."

"You boys might not believe me, and"—Mark got off the couch, wrapped in the blanket, and made his way to where they all stood—"you don't have any reason to believe me, but I do want what's best for you. I thought that was being with your mother, and I'm sorry I was wrong. But I know that your Uncle Matt won't ever let anything happen to you. You'll be happy here."

"But you'll visit us, like Vancy said?" Chris asked shyly.

"And call?" Ricky asked.

Mark knelt down, still wrapped in the blanket, and very solemnly nodded at the boys—his sons. "If you want me to, I'll call and visit you."

"We never had a dad," Chris said to Rick.

"The other kids did, but not us," Ricky agreed. "It might not be so bad, as long as you let us live with Uncle Matt."

"I will as long as you want," Mark promised.

"We want to live here forever," both boys said practically in sync.

"We want Vancy to live here too, but she won't. She's moving home." There was accusation in Ricky's words.

Vancy felt guilty but knew there was nothing she could do about it. They'd had enough seriousness this morning, so she tried to lighten the mood. "You're right, I have to move, but I'll visit a lot. I'll visit so much, you'll say, 'Oh, no, it's Vancy again.'"

They laughed. "No, we won't."

"That's what you say now, but what happens when you start school, and I say, 'Matt, I'll drive them.' Because you know if I drive you to school, I'll have to I kiss you good-bye. Your whole faces— all over," she teased, trying to sound ominous.

Neither boy was buying it. "We'll kiss you back."

"What if I wear lipstick and leave big kissy marks on your cheeks?"

That one stumped them. They looked at each other, then Chris said, "We'll tell the kids you're a witch and that those kissy marks mean we can't get turned into toads, but they don't have any, so they can."

"Yeah," Ricky said, obviously pleased with the story. "And they'll be scared."

This wasn't going in the direction Vancy had intended. "Okay, so maybe I won't kiss you with lipstick, because it's not nice to scare your friends."

"Hey, what do we call him?" Chris asked, pointing at Mark.

"What do you want to call him?" she asked them.

"Daddy?" Ricky asked softly.

"Mark?" Vancy asked, checking.

"Uh, that's fine, I guess." He stood. "I should probably get dressed now."

Vancy shooed the two boys toward the hall. "Okay, so why don't the two of you go get dressed too? We're going to drop you off at Nana Vancy's while your dad and Uncle Matt and I go to my office and get the papers signed."

"Nana Vancy!" they hooted, and they ran down the hall, leaving Vancy alone with the blanket-wrapped Mark.

"So what's the story between you and my brother?" he asked.

"We're friends," Vancy said simply, though there was no "simple" about it. What she felt for Matt went beyond friendship. "Now, why don't you get dressed as well? We've got a lot to do today."

Matt kept staring at his brother as they sat in Vancy's office. He was waiting for Mark to bolt or do something that would hold up the proceedings, but as Vancy and her lawyer friend, Jarrad, talked their legal mumbo jumbo, explaining what the papers meant, Mark just listened, nodded on occasion, and then, as Matt held his breath, signed the papers.

Jarrad, a nice enough seeming guy, got up. "It was nice meeting you both." He looked at Vancy. "You're back next week then?"

"Yes. And thanks for the help today. I'm better with business contracts, so this isn't my forte."

"No problem." He left the room.

The three of them sat for an uncomfortable

moment. Vancy wasn't sure what to say, and, obviously, neither was Matt or Mark.

Mark was the first one to crack under the weight of the silence. "Well, it's official." He stood, pushing back his chair. "Why don't you drop me at your place before you pick up the boys and give them the good news."

"You're just going to leave without even telling them good-bye?" Vancy asked, following Matt and Mark to the office door.

Mark was ahead of her and didn't turn around, just nodded. "I thought it would be for the best."

"Mark," she said, and she waited. When he finally turned and made eye contact, she continued quietly. "Speaking as someone who was recently deserted in a very public way—someone who was left without a backward glance, an explanation, or a good-bye—I can assure you that it's not for the best. Well, maybe for you, but definitely not for the boys."

"I'm just trying to do the right thing for once in my life." Mark raked a hand through his hair. "I don't want to confuse them."

"Mark . . ." Matt started, then stopped.

Vancy waited, hoping he'd find the words, but he simply looked at her.

"Then stay over again," she said gently. "Spend the day with them. Let them know something about you, then tell them why you're leaving them."

"Tell them I'm a screwup, that everything I touch crashes and burns?" He shook his head. "That the last thing they want is a father like me?"

"No, tell them you've got problems of your own that you need to take care of before you're able to take care of anyone else," Vancy tried.

"What kind of problems will make my leaving sound any better? Any suggestions? Do I tell them I louse up everything I touch?"

"Everyone has problems. You could go talk to someone," Vancy tried.

"Don't try to psychoanalyze me, princess, or send me to someone else who'll have a go at it. It won't work. I had a great childhood, parents who loved me, good schools, plenty of food on my plate each night. I was lucky."

"What about Matt?" He stood silently next to her, his face an unreadable mask. "You have a brother."

"I had that too, but I screwed that up as well, didn't I, Matt?"

"No matter what I say, you're out to make me the bad guy." Matt looked at Vancy. "Don't bother trying. He's going to do what he wants to do, just like he always has. I'll wait for you outside."

He walked out of the room and slammed the door.

"Yeah, poor Matt has spent his life picking up the pieces after me. He said he was done, but here he goes again, riding to the rescue and playing the hero. Don't get me wrong, I know the boys' being with him is for the best, but . . ."

"It's hard," Vancy supplied.

He nodded. They stood in silence for a minute.

"He's always tried to do the right thing, you know." Mark looked out the window, and Vancy followed suit.

"He's a good man with a big heart."

"I hate that he's the good one. That doesn't leave me anywhere to go but down."

Vancy couldn't help it—she laughed. "Does that excuse work for you? Blaming Matt for being so good that you have to be the bad twin? I mean, I could pretend to play along if you like."

Mark shot her a rueful grin. "I can see why he likes you."

"Mark, maybe there's more to you than you think. You know, if you'd taken the boys away from Matt, you'd have broken his heart. He fell in love with them the minute he laid eyes on them. Letting him be a part of their lives is the greatest gift you've ever given him."

"And I'm glad I get to be part of their life." Matt stepped back into the room. "But don't think that means I want to exclude you."

"I thought you left," Mark said.

"I didn't get very far, so I was eavesdropping," he said with no guilt. "Listen, Mark, the boys need you. Right now, you're not in a place to take care of them full-time, and I am. That's all well and good, but by giving me the legal right to do it doesn't mean you're not their father, that they don't need you and want to know you. That someday you might be in the position to take care of them."

"But if I did, what about you?"

"I'll still be their Uncle Matt. I'll always be their Uncle Matt, and as such, I want what's best for them. But you're their father, Mark. They need you."

"I've never held a job for more than a couple weeks."

"You lasted a lot longer than that with me."

Mark shrugged. "I liked it, but eventually . . . well, it doesn't matter."

"There's a job waiting for you if you want to try again."

Mark shook his head. "I don't think our working together is a good idea."

"I think I could get you a job at Salo Construction," Vancy offered. She never pulled strings, but she would this once. For Mark. No, if she was honest with herself, it would be for Matt. "Do you know anything about—"

"He's a certified plumber," Matt offered.

That surprised her. "You are? Then why—?"

"I don't take orders very well. One school psychiatrist said I had authority issues."

"Issues aren't terminal," Vancy told him. "You could learn to cope. You remind me of my sister, Dori, who doesn't just have authority issues, she bucks the status quo whenever an opportunity presents itself. Remind me to tell you about the time she wore a tux to the first grown-up party we were allowed to attend, rather than the ball gown my grandmother had bought her. She understands bucking the system."

"Why would you help me, princess?" Mark looked suspicious.

"You're Matt's brother, and Chris and Ricky's father. And I know what it's like to feel lost and have someone toss you a lifeline, so I'm tossing, but that's all I'm doing. It's up to you if you catch it."

"I'm not a good risk."

"I'll take my chances."

Mark smiled at her. There was nothing sarcastic about it, just a genuine expression. He turned to Matt. "You won't mind if I see the boys?"

"I'd mind if you didn't."

"Okay, then." He looked at Vancy. "I'll let you vouch for me, but I'd like to be hired on my own merits."

"Done."

Vancy hadn't been sure what to expect when they picked up the boys, but it seemed rather anticlimactic. They all went out to Steak and Shake for lunch, then took a trip to Erie's peninsula, Presque

Isle. They hadn't brought the boys' swimsuits, so they all kicked off their shoes and walked along the water's edge, barefoot.

Matt watched Vancy and the boys as they ran ahead.

"I can see why you love her," Mark said. "If you didn't, I might make a play for her myself."

Matt didn't ask how Mark knew, he simply said, "Is it that obvious?"

"I don't think she knows yet. But if I were you, I wouldn't wait too long to tell her."

"I was about to do that last night, when you showed up." He laughed. "You always did have impeccable timing."

Vancy and the boys were kneeling close to the tree line, looking at something. Matt moved toward them, Mark on his heels.

". . . and do you know what all these ants do? They look after one another. They're a big family. Aunts, uncles, sisters, brothers—"

"Grandmas and grandpas too?" Chris asked.

"Yep. They all take care of one another. All of them need each other."

"Like me and Chris, right? You and Uncle Matt and Nana Vancy and Papa Bela and our new grandpa and grandma—"

"And our dad too," Chris added.

"Yeah. You all take care of us."

Matt watched as Vancy put an arm around each

boy. "That's right. You've got a family. A big one. And our job—all of our jobs—is to take care of you."

"Not like our mom." There was a flatness in Ricky's voice.

"Your mom did take care of you, in her own way. She sent you to us because she knew she couldn't take care of you alone. Look at all those ants. Sometimes it takes a lot of people to take care of one another. She sent you to us."

"'Cause she couldn't do it alone?" Chris said.

"Right," Vancy assured them. "Someday she might come back, and you just remember that she sent you to us because she wanted what was best for you."

Both boys nodded, and they all got up. Vancy looked surprised when she spotted Matt and Mark. But he wasn't surprised at all. Wasn't surprised by her amazing ability to care for the boys, to give them something to hold on to about their mother.

He held her back as the boys ran with Mark to the water's edge. "I want to talk to you later."

"Sure. We can talk when you drive me home."

Matt just nodded, hoping by the time he drove her home, he could find some way to express all he felt.

Chapter Ten

The day ended too soon. They all got home from the beach, and Vancy tucked the boys in for their nap one last time. Her heart broke as she hugged them both. She knew it was absurd. She wasn't saying good-bye forever. She'd see them again often. But it wouldn't be the same.

She didn't want to leave, and she knew that was one of the biggest reasons she had to.

"I'm all packed," she told Matt as she came out of the office, her suitcase in one hand. "Can you drive me home now?"

Matt was standing in the living room, looking out the front window. He'd been quiet. Too quiet. "Matt?"

He turned and looked startled to see her standing there, suitcase in hand. "Sure. Let's go. You'll be okay?" he asked Mark, who was on the couch.

"I might be a screwup, but I think I can handle two sleeping boys."

Matt nodded and opened the door, holding it for Vancy.

"Mark, I left you the air mattress in Matt's office. I put fresh sheets on it. I thought it might be more comfortable than the couch."

"Thanks."

"I'll talk to Dori tomorrow, and we'll give you a call." She was stalling. She knew she was, just as she knew she had to go.

"I don't know how to thank you . . . how I'm going to repay you." He got up off the couch and hugged her. "Thanks."

"Just make it work this time—if not for your own sake, then for the boys'."

"I can't promise anything other than I'll try."

"That's enough for me." She forced herself to move toward the door.

Matt took her suitcase and wordlessly carried it out to the truck.

She followed suit, got in and got situated, and still he didn't say anything. He didn't start the truck. Just sat there looking out the window.

"So, are you going to ignore me the whole way back to my house?" She didn't say *home* because she realized that it felt as if she were leaving home, not going to it.

He just sat in the driver's seat and still didn't turn the ignition. "I just don't know what to say."

"Maybe you could start with telling me what's wrong."

He turned to her. "You swoop into my life like some Mary Poppins, putting everything in order, and then just disappear again."

"I'm not disappearing. I've got a life I've got to get back to." She could say all the right words, but she didn't believe them. Nothing in her wanted to leave here. Leave the boys.

Leave Matt.

"I know." He looked as frustrated as she felt. "And I know that my feeling as if you're abandoning me doesn't make sense."

"Feelings don't have to make sense. I know that better than most people do," she assured him.

"You know when you told Mark that I fell in love with the boys at first sight?"

"Yes. I could see it that first day. You didn't know you even had nephews, but you loved them. The kind of love that would make you do anything for someone. You've thrown your whole life upside down to take care of them. You're a special man, Matt Wilde."

"I never believed that kind of thing happened. But you're right, it did. I'd lay down my life for those boys. I'll do whatever it takes to keep them happy and safe."

She nodded. "I know that."

"I'm giving my brother another chance for them, even after I swore I was done with him."

She snorted. "You can tell yourself that if it makes you feel better, but it's a lie. You're giving Mark another chance because that's just how you are. You love with all your heart. No matter how many times he screws up, you'll always be there to offer him help, no matter what you say."

"We're getting off track. I was talking about believing in love at first sight now."

"I do understand. I fell for them just as hard. I may need to get back to work, but that doesn't mean I'm abandoning them. I plan to visit as often as you'll allow."

"Well, about that. That's sort of what I wanted to talk to you about."

Her heart did a little jump with what she was pretty sure was pure, unadulterated joy. "Did the day care fall through? I'm sure I can work out some at-home days. I could go into the office a few days a week, then do work from home the other days. Between that and Nana, who I'm sure will help, we can cover this. I didn't want to say anything, but I hated the thought of the boys going to day care. They should be with their family, with people who love them."

"Vancy, this isn't about day care. It's about love at first sight."

She tried not to feel disappointed that the day care plans hadn't fallen through. "Yeah, love at first sight. I know, we both fell for them."

"You," he said, clearly and distinctly, then said nothing else.

"You?" she asked, confused.

"You. I didn't just fall for them. I fell in love with *you*. I know you're still recovering from Al, and I know you need time to heal, and I'm willing to wait. I'd do anything to spend the rest of my life with you. But—"

He didn't get any further than that because Vancy had moved across the seat and was kissing him. "Yes," she said when they'd separated.

"Yes?" he parroted, confused.

She pulled back a bit from his embrace and looked him in the eye. "Well, wasn't that a marriage proposal?"

"Did you want it to be?" he asked.

"I did say yes, didn't I?" She was grinning.

Matt knew he was as well. He hugged her to him. "Well, then, yes, it was a marriage proposal."

The future rolled out in Matt's mind's eye. Years with Vancy, with Chris and Rick. With both their crazy families. And maybe with more children someday. He kissed her again, sealing the agreement. She'd said yes. Then he realized what she hadn't said. "You didn't say if you loved me too."

He needed to hear her say the words.

"Matthew Wilde, I love you. It's fast, but it's true. I had a hard time believing in my feelings for you, but you're right. If we can both believe we fell in love with two little boys at first sight, why should it be any harder to believe we could fall for each other that fast?" Then she laughed, not because either of them had said anything funny, but because she was so full of happiness, she had to let some spill over.

"Speaking of fast, how long do you think it will take you to plan the wedding?" Matt asked.

"What's the nearest state that has no waiting period for their marriage licences?"

"That fast? Are you sure? I don't want you to think I coerced you so soon after Al—"

"Who?" She smiled.

"The man you were going to marry."

She shook her head and held his hand in hers. "I'm afraid you're mixed up. The man I'm going to marry is named Matthew Wilde."

"Well, maybe we can convince Mark to babysit, and we can hop a plane to somewhere and get married tonight."

"That sounds like a plan."

"You're sure you won't feel you missed out on a big wedding like you'd planned?"

"As long as I'm your wife, I won't have missed out on anything."

She kissed him again because she could . . . because she loved him and he loved her.

All of a sudden there was movement outside the car and a bunch of blinding lights.

"Oh, no."

The press had found her. "Vancy Salo? Vancy, does this mean the curse is broken? That you and your ex are back together?"

She got out of the truck and faced the reporters. "Not quite. But I do have a story for you. It's about a bride-to-be whose grandmother cursed her own family so that no one would get a perfect wedding. You see, that grandmother was sensible enough not to curse them to lives without love. The bride-to-be thought she'd planned for every contingency, but it turned out she ended up losing the groom. Then, quite unexpectedly, she met the groom she was destined to have. The man she loved. And she realized that the curse wasn't really a curse for her. It was a blessing. . . ."

She went on and gave the media the whole story. She didn't mind their knowing that Vancy Salo, a woman who not too long ago had a huge, elaborate wedding planned—a wedding that had everything, everything but a groom, thanks to her grandmother's curse—now had the man she knew she was destined to spend the rest of her life with. And she knew that now she truly did have everything.

A life with a man she loved more than life itself.

Epilogue

*G*randmother's Curse Might Have Been Granddaughter's Salvation.

Nana Vancy reread the paper's article for the
hundredth time. "I'm famous," she murmured to
nobody but herself.

She looked at the happy couple dancing in
Vancy's backyard. She'd helped Mary Jane and
Marcy set up this impromptu family reception to
celebrate Matt and Vancy's marriage.

"Nana, is something wrong?" Noah asked.

"If your sister would have waited a bit longer so
we could plan another wedding, she could have
broken the curse, because she obviously didn't
care more about her wedding than about Matt."

"Nana, we've all told you over and over again,

there is no curse. Even the newspapers agreed that your 'curse' turned out to be Vancy's blessing. I never saw her look at Al the way she does at Matt. But I can promise you, I don't care what Julianna does for our wedding, so I'll break the curse for you."

"Julianna will care." Nana Vancy wasn't going to be wooed out of her glumness or believe that the curse was ready to stop torturing her.

Julianna walked over to Noah, who wrapped his arms around his fiancée. "Julianna, honey, tell Nana that the wedding doesn't matter to you. That being my wife is all that counts."

"I've always known I'd marry Noah," Julianna assured her.

"So how you marry him doesn't matter?" she asked, feeling a surge of hopefulness.

"Not at all, Nana."

"Then maybe you'd let me plan the wedding? I mean, if you just sit back and don't worry about it, then it's obvious that you care more about the marriage, and the curse will have to be broken, won't it?"

Julianna kissed her cheek. "Plan away."

"Really?"

"Truly."

Noah wrapped his arms around his fiancée again, and Vancy Balshade Salo watched Noah and Julianna join Matt and Vancy on the dance floor.

She wanted to believe that ending the curse was that simple.

But her mother used to say, "Don't count your storks until they've landed on the house." She'd plan the wedding and hope for the best.

But she wouldn't worry about that until tomorrow. Today was a day for celebrating.

"Come on, Bela, you old goat. You owe me a dance."